Anonymous

**The County**

Vol. II

Anonymous

**The County**
*Vol. II*

ISBN/EAN: 9783337054366

Printed in Europe, USA, Canada, Australia, Japan

Cover: Foto ©Andreas Hilbeck / pixelio.de

More available books at **www.hansebooks.com**

# THE COUNTY

# THE COUNTY

*A NOVEL*

IN TWO VOLUMES

VOL. II.

LONDON
SMITH, ELDER, & CO., 15 WATERLOO PLACE
1889

[*Reprinted from the 'Cornhill Magazine'*]

# CONTENTS

OF

## THE SECOND VOLUME

# THE COUNTY

## CHAPTER XXII

### VISITORS

As we enter the house we find Fra
ing over the hall fire, and even i
of my own suppressed agitation I
by the pale face she turns towar
her big blue eyes dilate as exci
sight of Sir Allan Vaudrey as if
quondam lover of her own who h
made his appearance.

Their greeting is effusive in t
a fact which somewhat surprises
moment, as they never used to be
to one another. However, I

known that well-invested millions constitute
a claim upon respect which Frances would
be the last person to ignore ; and Sir Allan
for his part will apparently embark upon a
new estimate of her character on the ground
that her vices have originated in proximity to
me, whereas her virtues must be all her own.

'Your house is charming, positively
charming,' declares Mrs. Stuart. 'You always
had exquisite taste, and I suppose it has been
given free play. What delicious old leather !
May I have a peep at the other rooms before
lunch ? '

And so she carries me off, whispering as
soon as we are out of earshot, ' It *was* Frances
who was his ancient flame, was it not ? I
used always to try and find out, but he had a
very baffling way of pretending to admire you
both, while decidedly giving me the impression
that it was Frances whom he preferred. I
think it is most *empressé* on his part to come
about her so quickly after getting his money ;

and you know it was at his own hint that I asked him to stay with me just now—though indeed I am always delighted to have him ! '

' That is the morning-room and this is the white library,' I answer, with inapposite stiffness; 'which will you see first?' And I walk into the library without waiting for a reply.

' Delightful! Too delightful! One becomes a long note of admiring exclamation in looking at your rooms. And what period is this? It *is* a period, I am sure, because it all looks so quaint and out of the common. Ah! How pleased you would be to see Frances settled down near you in just such another house as this! He would have to buy a place in one of the habitable counties, of course, for she would never dream of living at that terrible barn of old Sir Joshua's near the business.'

' Don't you think we are getting on a little too fast?' I inquire, endeavouring vainly to infuse some jocosity into a voice which only sounds indignant.

'Oh, I don't know! When the two parties " are willin'" everything else follows so quickly nowadays.'

I don't think Mrs. Stuart can have improved lately. Her voice used surely not to be so loud and harsh ; and her features look quite coarse in the morning light. She always was in the habit of calling a spade a spade, but I really consider it positively indelicate the way her imagination is running riot to-day.

'Well, you must have spent a mint of money,' she concludes, as I pilot her back to the inner hall, where Frances, in one of her most fetching attitudes, is leaning against the high back of a carved oak chair, and making eyes at Sir Allan.

'Poetry!' cries Mrs. Stuart. 'Now, it is no use denying it; my ears are sharp. You were quoting some tender lines to that young man, Miss Frances.'

'They weren't *very* tender,' returns Frances, with another arch *œillade*; 'but Sir Allan is so modest that I don't fancy he would like me to repeat them.'

'Ha, ha!' laughs Sir Allan. 'Yes, say them again, Miss Frances, do.'

The hard look has gone from his face, and he is beaming genially under Frances' blandishments. It is positively painful how even the best of men like talking about themselves, and my sister on the war-path has but two themes, herself and himself, capable, indeed, of much preluding and endless variations, but ever hovering around the engrossing topics.

> 'How much a dunce that has been sent to roam
> Excels a dunce that has been kept at home,'

quotes Frances, on being thus pressed 'R-o-a-m, the poet means—not the capital of Italy; r-o-a-m, which may imply India or any other appropriate place.'

'H'm! I call your verses very tender,'

declares Mrs. Stuart. 'What do you say,
Mrs. Mansfield?'

'I don't read much poetry, so I am not a
fair judge,' I return coldly.

'Mrs. Mansfield rises superior to the
foolish twitterings of the bards,' says Sir Allan
mockingly, and Frances chimes in—

'She always was a practical little soul,
weren't you, darling?'

The noise of the luncheon-gong prevents
any further analysis of my character, and
Bryan appears at the same moment.

The greeting between Allan Vaudrey and
my husband is of the most cursory, though I
notice a red flush mount to Allan's forehead
as they shake hands—for Mrs. Stuart immediately absorbs all Bryan's attention.

He did not know her before, but she has
a masonic 'hail-fellow-well-met' manner with
men which in two minutes establishes her in
their innermost affection.

She is a peer's daughter, too, and what

well-constituted British mind is indifferent to that halo?

'It is really kind of you to come and see us in this sociable way,' I overhear Bryan expatiating to her at a very early stage of lunch. 'I must say that most of my wife's old friends have not received her as cordially as she had a right to expect.'

Mrs. Stuart's voice is not so audible as usual in reply. She is apparently disconcerted at this unexpected confidence, and mumbles something confusedly about county people being proverbially slow.

'That, of course, is well known, and most justifiable with regard to strangers,' agrees Bryan with impartial severity, 'but it ought not to apply in Esmé's case. Her birth and my means deserve a more decided recognition.'

'Ah, but do we ever get our deserts in this world? I doubt it,' rejoins Mrs. Stuart cheerfully—it would take more than even Bryan is capable of to put her out of counten-

ance for long.   'Look at me, for instance.   I
am sure that I *deserve* the stud of a potentate
of the turf, and here I am beginning the
hunting season with one elderly nag.'

'Then I hope you will allow me to have
the pleasure of mounting you occasionally,'
says Bryan, exactly as if he were offering her
a glass of water.   'We will inspect the stables
after lunch, and you can choose your own
animal.'

Mrs. Stuart is oftener on the back of someone else's steed than her own, and does a good
bit of horse-broking in a quiet way by riding
dealers' horses, and getting them sold in consequence of their wonderful achievements
under her clever manipulation.   I have also
known her accept mounts at the hands of
widely-varying individuals, from the Master
down to sporting farmers—but I don't think
she will take one from Bryan.

'It is most kind of you, Mr. Mansfield, to
think of such a thing, but please don't men-

tion the subject again. I was only joking, of course, and I ride my husband's horses when I have none of my own.'

Having thus extricated herself, Mrs. Stuart steals an awkward glance at me, to find out whether I am listening to this pleasing conversation, and is much relieved to see that, to all appearance, I am absorbed in the account Frances is giving Sir Allan of Riverdale society.

'Yes, I dare say there were some decent people within reach—within ten miles, for instance,' she is saying; 'but then you see Sir Joseph did not care to have anything to do with them. No disinterested person would assume the grovelling attitude which he expects from his fellow beings, so of course he is dependent upon the village for society.'

'Well, at any rate, you have done with him now, I suppose,' returns Sir Allan half inquiringly.

'Yes, indeed; my fondest hope is never to

set eyes upon him or any other Riverdalian again,' says Frances calmly.

I flush with shame at her heartlessness and want of nice feeling in speaking so contemptuously of Sir Joseph before other people; whatever his failings may be, he has been very good to her.

'Then your fondest hope is doomed to disappointment,' I cry hotly. 'I have always intended to write and ask the Yarboroughs to come and stay with us as soon as we are settled.'

'I believe I have heard you say so,' answers my sister coolly; 'but before that letter is posted there will be a pitched battle royal between your high and mightiness and your humble servant. Why, you will be asking Uncle Frank and Priestman next!'

'By the way, how are your Uncle Frank and Mrs. Nugent?' asks Sir Allan. 'Do you ever hear anything about them?'

'Oh yes, no end of stories,' answers

Frances laughing ; ' our new aunt is a clever creature. I always did admire her tact. They say she has made Billington a perfect Temple of the Creature Comforts, with Uncle Frank as deity and herself as high priestess.'

' I can imagine it,' ejaculates Sir Allan, ' and nothing is withheld from the altar, I suppose ? '

'Nothing,' echoes Frances. ' We hear through the servants that the drawing-room reeks of tobacco and that Uncle Frank's Dandie Dinmont sleeps upon the billiard table. They say that odious little cases of liqueur and stands of brandy and soda are stuck about all over the house, so that Uncle Frank may help himself at any moment without the exhausting toil of ringing the bell, and that he lives from one week's end to the other in a dirty old velveteen smoking-coat which we took away from him ages ago, and which Priestman unearthed directly they came home from the honeymoon.'

'I don't know why you call the woman clever,' remarks Allan contemptuously ; ' she seems to be leading the life one might expect from a servant turned mistress, and your uncle is letting himself down to her level.'

'Ah, you haven't heard all yet,' cries Frances ; ' she encourages Uncle Frank in his lazy ways, but she is active enough herself. She has gone through a course of theological reading under the auspices of the Brackham dissenting minister—this was after she found out that the vicar's wife didn't mean to call—and has finally become a Plymouth Sister.'

'A Plymouth Sister,' repeats Allan, con-siderably puzzled ; ' but why ? '

'Far be it from me to impute interested motives to so serious a proceeding,' says Frances ; 'still it strikes one as a curious coincidence that Priestman's conversion should have taken place just as old Lord Sandilands was dying. His cousin, who succeeds to the title, and whose place adjoins Billington, is a rabid Plymouth Brother.'

'Yes, Priestman and the new Lady Sandilands are already hand in glove,' I strike in.

But Allan pays no attention to me. He is gazing contemplatively at Frances. It is scarcely likely that he has come across so radiant a face during his travels in the sun-scorched East, but it is not polite to ignore his hostess so completely as he is doing, even to impress a complexion of lilies and roses and features of child-like sweetness upon his mind.

'Surely you have grown taller since I saw you last, Miss Nugent,' he says suddenly, and I start at my old name from his lips. In the dear old days I used always to be 'Miss Nugent,' and she 'Miss Frances;' but he seems quite callous to the change.

'Do you think so?' she says dubiously. 'One does not grow at nineteen.'

'Nineteen, is it?' asks Sir Allan, bending forward with a smile.

'Still truthfully nineteen,' returns Frances solemnly; 'but I will tell you a secret. Next week it will be twenty—and after that never more than twenty, not if you ask me again in ten years' time.'

'There is nothing like fixing an age and sticking to it,' assents Sir Allan; 'but I think twenty is rather early to begin.'

I crumble my bread impatiently and look out of the window. Sir Allan and Frances are sitting one on each side of me, and, unless I force my way into a conversation where I am evidently not wanted, there is nothing to do but attend to my lunch and listen meekly.

'You are going to the Brackham ball, of course?' asks Sir Allan presently.

'Of course,' replies Frances. 'Not to go to the Brackham ball is looked upon in these parts as equivalent to a confession that one is ill either in body, mind, or pocket.'

Then why was she so anxious this morning to go up to town for the next ten days? I

wonder. She remembers her own inconsis-
tency before the words are out of her mouth,
I think, for she colours a little, and looks up
to see if I have noticed her slip.

'Yes, I know that everyone turns out for
it,' says Sir Allan. 'I went with you two
years ago from Billington, if you remember.'
And with the last words he turns and looks at
me with a wrathful look.

If I remember !

'Esmé, what was the price of that brocade
stuff in the wall-panels of your boudoir?' asks
Bryan across the table. 'Mrs. Stuart admires
these curtains very much, but I tell her they
are nothing compared with some of the things
about the house. Did not the material I am
speaking of cost a guinea a foot?'

'I really forget what it cost,' I exclaim,
rising suddenly from my seat. Frances is
still nibbling biscuits, and Bryan has not
finished his cheese, but I cannot sit here any
longer. Then, with the quick touch of

remorse which always comes over me when I have been rude to my husband, I add more gently, 'But if Mrs. Stuart takes any interest in it I shall be delighted to show her my boudoir.'

So we adjourn upstairs, Mrs. Stuart and I, Bryan following us. The attraction for him is twofold; he thinks Mrs. Stuart a most delightful woman, and he is as pleased as a child to exhibit his new toy. It has been a positive affliction to him that so few people have as yet been inside his house to be impressed by its splendours.

'Come into the hall with me,' says Frances to Sir Allan. 'You don't want to stare at brocade which cost a guinea a foot, do you?'

Apparently he does not; and on our return to the hall, half an hour afterwards (having minutely and exhaustively inspected boudoir, bedrooms, corridors, and having only refrained from cataloguing the glories of the lower regions through fear of disturbing the servants at their mid-day carousals), we find him contentedly lounging in one big armchair, while Frances, propped up with gorgeous cushions, harangues him from another.

'More poetry?' whispers Mrs. Stuart. 'And you told me before lunch that I was looking too far ahead! My dear, in your place, I should be thinking of a suitable gown in which to play the part of mother-sister at the wedding. Now, Sir Allan, I am sorry to rout you out, but we must be going.'

The roan cobs are brought round, and Mrs. Stuart is carefully packed in her pretty phaeton, with foot-muff and fur rug.

'Good-bye!' cries Frances from the doorstep, as Sir Allan gets in beside her and Bryan goes off to open the lawn gate. 'We shall look out for you at Knole Bridge if the frost breaks by Monday. Good-bye!'

Then dancing up to me as I stand gazing gloomily into the hall fire, she says gaily—

' I have taken him off your hands beauti-fully, haven't I, dear ? '

'You have indeed ! ' I respond, and turn ungratefully away.

# CHAPTER XXIII

## BILLS

'I THINK it would not be at all a bad plan to give a ball,' says Bryan reflectively, as he cracks a walnut at dessert that evening.

'A ball!' I exclaim with a start, aroused from a deep reverie in which I have been debating within myself the knotty point as to whether grief for his father and brother has alone sufficed to age Sir Allan Vaudrey's face and draw those weary lines around his eyes. ' Why, what do you want to give a ball for, Bryan?'

'I think it would improve our. position,' replies my husband.

'What do you mean by improving our position?' I ask, colouring impatiently.

'I suppose people would be obliged to call upon you afterwards if they came to your ball, would they not?' he inquires. 'Now, Lady Dromore, for instance—if you invited her, she would be obliged to call upon you?'

'Dear Bryan, people never do things like that in the country!' I exclaim, reddening more and more, as much from genuine disgust at the bare notion of my touting for Lady Dromore's patronage, as from annoyance that anyone, though it be only Frances, should hear my husband propose such a thing. 'I could not possibly invite people who have taken no notice of me since my marriage.'

'I don't think it would answer, really, Bryan,' says Frances, not at all hastily, but with cool consideration; she is not half so much shocked at the idea as I am. 'People do that sort of thing immensely in town, no doubt, but it would not go down here.'

'You don't think so?' queries Bryan.

'Mrs. Stuart seemed to fancy it would be a good plan.'

'You don't mean to say you asked her?' I cry.

'No, she suggested it. I was explaining to her how very rudely one or two ladies have treated you, and she said, " Why don't you give a ball? It is always a popular thing to do. Once when my brother was election-eering he gave a ball; " and then she went on to tell me some anecdotes about the people who came to it, but I did not think them very funny,' continued the unconscious Bryan.

'For Heaven's sake do impress upon him that if he really wants to "improve our position,"' says Frances, mimicking Bryan's voice as we make our way to the drawing-room, 'he must first learn to hold his tongue.'

'You can hint it delicately to him if you like,' I reply; 'I am sick of finding fault.'

'It is more than my place is worth,' declines Frances, shaking her head. 'He is not too fond of me as it is.'

Having reached the drawing-room, she ensconces herself comfortably in a low chair and settles her feet lazily upon the fender. Frances has a supreme contempt for the arts of the needle, or indeed for any occupation whatsoever, and manages to combine the *dolce far niente* very satisfactorily with a northern climate.

As I turn to the piano—Schumann's 'Warum?' is running through my head, and it will tally with the questions I should like to put to Fate—my sister stops me.

'You have not told me one word about your meeting with Allan Vaudrey,' she says reproachfully.

'There's nothing to tell,' I answer shortly, and sitting down, run my fingers over the keys of the piano.

'Well, I suppose you could scarcely rush

into one another's arms and exclaim, " My long-lost love ! " in Mrs. Stuart's presence,' agrees Frances indifferently.

' Scarcely. But you may as well give us credit for refraining from such a proceeding upon higher moral grounds, seeing that we did not meet in Mrs. Stuart's presence,' I murmur between the notes.

' No? ' says Frances, sitting up with suddenly aroused interest. ' How was that ? '

' Sir Allan was walking along the road by himself when I met him. Mrs. Stuart was in a cottage.'

And I begin softly—

but I get no farther, for Frances jumps up from her easy-chair, comes swiftly across the room, and lays a firm, detaining hand upon my wrist.

'He was walking by himself when you met him,' she repeats breathlessly. 'What did he say to you? What did you say to him? Quick, tell me before Bryan comes in!'

'Don't be so tragic, Frances!' I exclaim, half laughing, half angry. 'Really, to hear you talk one might imagine that I was the heroine of a French novel! What on earth *should* I say to Sir Allan, and he to me, except "How do you do?"'

'Didn't he refer to—to the last time he met you, and all that?' asks Frances incoherently.

'Not once. And I shall be much obliged' —making sudden demand upon my little stock of dignity—'if you will not imply that I have anything to tell you about Sir Allan Vaudrey which I should not wish Bryan to hear.'

As I make this highly respectable request my husband saunters into the room. There is an annoyed expression on his usually impassive face, and he holds in his hands a lengthy blue document of several sheets riveted together—on the face of it a bill of malignant character.

'Here's that tiresome fellow Curtis bothering me for money when his order isn't half completed,' he says disgustedly. 'I think I had better pitch his account into the fire and settle it that way.'

'But Curtis' order is completed, is it not?' I ask. 'Everything for the drawing-room was finished a month ago.'

'Ah! Well, it is for the drawing-room that he wants his money. He says he has been put to so much expense for "wall decoration, antique and inlaid furniture, and costly materials, out of the ordinary run, and therefore not kept in stock, that he will be most grateful for a remittance to enable him to

balance his cash-book!"' quotes Bryan, holding the accompanying letter from him as if
hydrophobia might ensue from closer contact.

'That sounds very reasonable,' say I,
leaving the piano and joining my husband on
the hearthrug; 'and he has executed the
order extremely well. What is the total,
Bryan?'

'Four thousand five hundred,' replies
Bryan.

'What!' I gasp. 'Four thousand five
hundred pounds for this one room. It is not
possible!'

'I am afraid it is,' returns Bryan; 'but
you may just as well look over it and see if
the items are correct.'

And, handing me the bill with an air of
relief, he drops into one of Mr. Curtis' easiest
chairs, and in ten minutes is napping quietly
behind the outspread sheets of "The Field."

'Good Heavens!' I ejaculate in pious
dismay as I survey the hideous row of figures,

standing against my embroidered velvet curtains.

'Good Heavens!' again, in monotonous horror, as I discover the exaggerated value Mr. Curtis attaches to that old Persian rug in the east window.

' " One escritoire, Louis XVI., reproduced from own French model, inlaid and mounted to correspond, &c., 315*l.*" Shocking! Three hundred guineas for that Brummagem imitation!

' " One *chaise longue*, mounted in genuine Louis XVI. brocade, bunches of flowers tied with blue ribbon on coffee-coloured ground, legs hand-made, and inlaid to correspond, 110*l.*" Frightful! How can I ever put my feet up on it again?

' " One easy-chair, mounted in——" '

'You will have the nightmare to-night if you go on like that,' breaks in Frances lazily from the self-same chair. 'What is the use of tormenting yourself over each item? I

suppose you knew what " the dem'd total," as
Mr. Mantalini says, would be.'

'Indeed I did not!' I cry eagerly. 'I
wanted to know the price of each thing as I
ordered it, but Bryan laughed so at the idea
that I could not get anything satisfactory
from Curtis.'

'Well, Bryan can afford it, can't he?'

'I dare say,' I answer, twisting my bill
uncomfortably ; 'but I don't like spending
such a sum of money on furniture when
there is so much misery and want in the
world.

'It's good for trade,' says Frances philosophically ; 'so it comes to the same thing in
the long run.'

'Fifty-seven pounds for the chair you are
sitting on,' I murmur reflectively ; 'and when
I thought of sending that child of Morgan's
to the deaf and dumb college to be properly
taught, I found I had not money enough to
pay for her outfit and entrance fee.'

'But you could have got it from Bryan, could you not?' inquires Frances sharply.

'I did not ask him,' I murmur evasively.

There is no need to tell Frances that I always find it very difficult to get ready money from Bryan, generous though he be in encouraging me to run up bills.

'I cannot understand that amateur pottering about with poor people,' muses Frances aloud. 'I can understand my namesake of Assisi, who did the thing with professional thoroughness, and literally gave up all that he had to the poor; but if you once begin to spend money on yourself I don't see the difference between paying fifty pounds or five for a chair. Giving tithes of all a man possesses seems to me the weakest of compromises.'

'But, Frances, it is better than giving nothing,' I remonstrate.

'I don't see any difference,' she repeats.

'It is only putting down so much superfluous cash for the luxury of a quiet conscience.'

Then leaning forward to poke the glowing coals—

'What an economical wife I should be in that respect,' she concludes; 'for I don't mind acknowledging that I have no conscience to be quieted!'

# CHAPTER XXIV

## IN SOCIETY

NEXT morning it is Frances who is restless and fidgety.

I have lapsed into silent thought, and am drearily rehearsing the sharp speeches, and sadly recalling the cruel glances so freely bestowed upon me yesterday by Sir Allan Vaudrey.

'After all, it serves me right for caring two straws how he looks or what he says, now that I am a married woman,' and I pull myself up with strait-laced propriety ; but somehow the stays of matrimonial duty do not stiffen my mental back with much efficacy, and presently I find myself again lamenting that Allan could not have given me the kindly greeting of a friend.

'He certainly has improved in wondrous fashion,' says Frances abruptly, pausing in one of her many flittings from window to door, and from room to room, to finger the shaded blue silks of my embroidery. She has deserted her lounge and her cushions this morning, and appears as bitten by the demon of unrest as I was two days ago.

'Who has improved?' I ask listlessly. 'Bryan?'

'Dutiful spouse!' returns my sister with a laugh. 'How right and proper to appropriate the pronoun "he" to Bryan! And how devoted you are becoming to "him!" But it was not your Bryan I was thinking of at that moment—it was Allan Vaudrey.'

And she half turns away, holding up two skeins to the light.

Something jars on me; a vague suspicion steals over me.

'Oh! You find Sir Allan Vaudrey improved, do you?' I inquire sharply. 'Well, there was room for improvement in your opinion of him.'

'Perhaps so,' answers Frances with a regretful sigh. 'But I was so anxious lest you should marry a poor man that I put all his little shortcomings under a microscope.'

'And now that your sisterly anxiety is removed, you see with clearer, juster eyes!' I finish scornfully.

Frances gives an uncomfortable twist of the shoulder nearest me.

'Have I not just said that I think him wonderfully improved? He is so much quieter and more dignified.'

'It is astonishing how suddenly two millions invest a man with dignity in some people's estimation,' I remark, with an angry jerk of the needle, and turning a wrathful glare upon Frances.

She meets it unflinchingly; she is not going to yield an inch; and her steady gaze says more than her words.

'Dear Esmé, you seem annoyed at my praising Sir Allan; and is it my fancy that you did not like our getting on so well together yesterday?'

'It is not fancy at all,' I cry. 'I certainly was disgusted to see you hurl yourself at the head of a man whom you have always loaded with abuse.'

'One lives and learns,' observes Frances coolly; 'and, as to the hurling, I think there was as much on his part as on mine.'

Silence for a while. Various crushing remarks are checked on the tip of my tongue by the determined recollection of those aforesaid matrimonial corsets, and I bend over a ridiculous blue rose, apparently absorbed in the monstrosities of its shading.

'It is not like you to be so dog in-themangery,' says Frances presently, in plaintive, infantine accents; that particular childish whine is usually reserved for the undoing of the sterner sex, and has certainly never before been assumed for my destruction.

'You have married a rich man yourself, and you are very fond of him now. I am sure you always jump down my throat if I say half a syllable against him—and you begrudge me your—well, your leavings!'

As she puts forth this extraordinary version of the case, the little glass door leading to the terrace is pushed open from outside, and Bryan enters, flushed and panting.

'Mrs. Stuart's groom has just ridden over with a note for you, Esmé; I took it from him in the stable-yard and ran round the laurel walk with it; I thought you would get it quicker that way.'

He mops his brow—it does not require much exertion to make Bryan hot—and looks around for applause.

'It is sure to be an invitation, you see,' he adds in excited explanation. 'Open it quickly, like a good girl.'

As I take the tiny scissors from my work-basket and cut the flap of the envelope I rummage hurriedly in my mind for some pretext which will prevent me at least from lunching, dining, or partaking of any other feast in the combined company of Sir Allan Vaudrey, Bryan, and Frances; but nothing which would bear investigation occurs to me on the spur of the moment, and I pull out Mrs. Stuart's note, Frances looking over my shoulder with sisterly familiarity.

'Well?' asks Bryan breathlessly.

'Invitation to dinner to-morrow evening,' returns Frances with triumphant brevity.

'Ah—h!' and Bryan draws a long breath of intensest satisfaction.

'I wonder who will be there?' he speculates presently.

'She mentions the Dromores and Mr.

Mostyn,' answers Frances, picking up the note as I put it down.

' Just the very people we wanted to meet,' declares Bryan, his cup of delight indeed overflowing. 'Hadn't you better go and answer it at once, Esmé dear; or shall I bring your writing things here ? '

' H'm ! ' I cough dubiously. ' It is very short notice.'

Bryan's face falls.

' So it is,' he says disconcertedly ; ' but after all we can't afford to be too particular.'

' There is no doubt that she sent the note over by hand because she got a refusal from someone else by this morning's post,' I continue, ' hope springing eternal in my breast,' though I am genuinely sorry to throw cold water upon Bryan's delight ; he is as easily played upon as a child.

' I am afraid it looks like it,' he responds dismally ; ' but I *should* like to meet——'

' How can you be so absurd, Esmé ? '

strikes in Frances angrily. ' Why, Mrs.
Stuart distinctly says the whole thing has
been got up quickly.'

' It is very easy to say that!' I scoff;
' and——'

' Does she say that? ' eagerly exclaims
Bryan at the same instant.

'Of course she does!' returns Frances.
' She says she asked one or two people out
hunting yesterday, and is sending off to you
by the first opportunity.'

Foiled upon this tack, I then suggest, as
artfully as in me lies, that Frances and Bryan
shall go without me—that it looks a little
*empressé* for all three of us to present ourselves the first time we are asked ; that I
fancy I have a cold coming on ; and finally,
that it would be kinder not to burden Mrs.
Stuart with a superfluous woman in a neighbourhood where the nobler sex is so rare.

But in vain. I am routed all along the
line. Bryan refuses to appear without me ;

Frances points out that I can, if necessary, wear my pansy velvet, which is high to the throat; and both vociferate that Mrs. Stuart has always a crowd of men at her beck and call. So, the next evening we file into Mrs. Stuart's drawing-room—two white-robed women (the pansy velvet, strange to say, was not required), and one black-garbed man.

*A propos* of those black garments, I, for my part, am heartily grateful for the oft and much-abused fashion which prescribes the self-same evening attire for all mankind— royalty and waiters inclusive. How vastly would my discomfort in society be increased if, in addition to the perpetual anxiety with which I bate my breath at each remark of Bryan's, I were also tormented with the uneasy consciousness that his trousers were of the wrong material, and his waistcoat three shades brighter than any other man's?

I am sure, if the sighed-for last century

costume were really to come in again, Bryan's taste in waistcoats would be terribly florid!

'So sweet of you to come,' welcomes Mrs. Stuart. 'We have been pining for you ever since our last meeting. Haven't we, Sir Allan?'

'I beg your pardon,' says Sir Allan. He is just shaking hands with Bryan, and looks very tall and particularly stiff. 'I didn't catch what you said.'

'I said we had been pining for their society,' with a sweep of her fan towards us. 'Of course I meant that I had been pining for Mrs. Mansfield and Miss Nugent, and you for Mr. Mansfield. Far be it from me to make any more compromising statement!'

On a sofa just behind Mrs. Stuart are seated Lady Dromore and Mrs. Westby. They are both perfectly cognisant of my presence. While apparently absorbed in thrilling conversation they have taken in every detail of my gown; they have priced the diamonds of the big crescent in my hair —I am not spattered all over with odds and ends of brooches, but the few stones I have on will bear inspection—and they are at present occupied with my *balayeuse*, which is of real old Mechlin.

'How d' do?' exclaims Mr. Mostyn, starting forward from that chosen spot so mysteriously dear to the masculine heart —the hearthrug. 'Glad to see you back again.'

The pack of hounds which delight the neighbourhood are Mr. Mostyn's, and are kept up at his own expense. Holy and righteous is he who spareth his neighbour's pocket!

But not for this alone is Mr. Mostyn so universally popular. He has never been known to do or say a nasty thing. It may be true that he does nothing but hunt, and rarely says anything at all; still there are occasions when it appears that he is not unconscious of all that goes on around him ; and just now, as he stands beside me, twitching his shoulders nervously and racking his brains for conversation, I am fully aware that he means to demonstrate on my behalf as clearly as in him lies.

'I heard you were out the other day,' he goes on jerkily, ' but I didn't see you.'

'There was such a mob,' I respond, glancing over his shoulder in the direction of the door, where Sir Allan is still. employed in greeting Frances. I think she must be telling him what trouble she had to get me here, for her eyebrows are arched under her fringe, and her pretty mouth is pursed up in mock tribulation.

'Yes, it leaked out that the Prince was coming,' says Mr. Mostyn, standing first on one leg and then on the other.

Dinner is announced, and Lady Dromore sails past on Mr. Stuart's arm. 'How do you do?' she says grudgingly as she passes me, yellow as a guinea and stupid as a turkey.

Allan and Frances are parted now, for to him falls the honour of taking in Mrs. Westby —to such giddy heights will a baronetcy lead one! But Frances catches them up at the dining-room door, and pilots herself into the seat on his left hand.

We are eleven, and Bryan is the odd man. As he drifts uncomfortably in all alone, and stands looking for a vacant place, I draw Mr. Mostyn a little further down the table, and leave a chair for Bryan by him. Mr. Mostyn is the kindest person here.

'No, I didn't stay in Paris,' says Sir Allan, in answer to some remark from Mrs. Westby. 'I am afraid the charms of Paris are rather thrown away upon me, for I can't speak French.'

'Ah, that is a great defect in the education of the modern Englishman,' sighs Mrs. Westby, wagging her head sorrowfully—and such a plain little head it is to wag! A turnip might envy its roundness and lack of features. 'I do my best to remedy it in the case of my own boys by always talking French to them in their holidays.'

'Awfully good of you to take so much trouble,' replies Allan absently; though my eyes are lifted in appropriate attention to Mr. Mostyn, who is running over the meets for next week, I am perfectly well aware that Allan has been scanning me critically ever since we sat down to dinner. 'It must be a great bore.'

'Not at all,' says Mrs. Westby affectedly. 'I am obliged to keep up my French for the ambassadors, you know.'

'For the ambassadors?' repeats Sir Allan in a puzzled tone. He is evidently wondering much what high diplomatic female has fallen to his lot this evening.

'Yes, it is so necessary to speak French well to put them entirely at their ease!'

'Hawley on Friday and Baker's Mill on
Saturday,' finishes Mr. Mostyn. 'Shall you
be out on Saturday? We are sure to draw
some of the Billington coverts.'

'I don't know,' I reply hesitatingly. 'I
have not been near the old place yet.'

'It is naturally very trying for Mrs. Mansfield,' strikes in Bryan, from Mr. Mostyn's left
side. 'Billington was so nearly being her own,
you see.'

'Oh! er—er.' Mr. Mostyn is not a man
of many words, and a sudden conversational
attack is apt to find him unprepared; but he
means to be civil, and turns half round towards my husband.

'Her father was the eldest brother, you
may remember,' continues Bryan explanatorily
to the man whose acres run parallel with those
of Billington for many a mile, and who was at
school and college with my father; 'and if
she had only been a boy it would have been
all right. Both she and her sister have names

that would do just as well for boys—Esmé
and Frances. It must have been a great disappointment to them all.'

'Well, *you* ought not to regret it;' and
Mr. Mostyn is so pleased with his own joke
that he breaks out into a hearty laugh.

'Oh no! I don't regret it, of course,'
replies Bryan, with the air of a man who can
afford it. 'Land is a poor sort of investment
nowadays, and people who have no other resources must go to the wall.'

Mr. Mostyn's property being entirely
agricultural, he can scarcely be expected
to assent very cheerfully to this proposi-
tion.

On the other side of the table Frances has
rescued Allan from Mrs. Westby's grip,
which, to do that lady justice, was speedily
relaxed for an attack upon Lord Dromore,
when she found from one or two leading
remarks that Allan's heart was not in the
right place, and that he was totally indifferent

to what the Prince ate for luncheon the other day.

Do my ears deceive me, or do I hear Frances murmuring gently, 'It must be deeply interesting to own a township and works where so many human beings are employed. How much good you will be able to do!'

'You see it is so frightfully difficult in all such cases to give help and improve the condition of these poor people without pauperising them,' returns Allan.

How quickly she has mounted him on his hobby! It is evidently still his hobby, for he has passed two entrées, and has turned round to her with a new alertness in his bearing.

'Of course, of course,' with rapt, upturned countenance and saint-like absorption. 'It is quite a problem of political economy, is it not?'

'Yes,' nods Allan. 'But what do you care about paupers and political economy?' with sudden suspicion. 'I should fancy that neither you nor your sister thought twice about anything but——' And he pauses, uncertain how far his resentment may express itself with due regard to the proprieties.

'Of anything but ourselves, you mean,' sighs Frances, with meekly drooping head.

'Of yourselves and your clothes—and your diamonds,' says Allan bitterly.

Now Frances naturally has no diamonds and I have; therefore I am afraid it is not Frances to whom he is referring. Some intuition of this probably inspires her to reply with gentle humility—

'Yes, it is terrible how one is influenced by habit and—and—one's surroundings! But indeed you wrong me in thinking that I do not care.'

I lose the rest, for Bryan here leans across Mr. Mostyn and me to offer the address of his wine merchant to our host. 'First-rate fellow!' he declares solemnly. 'And a baronet's cousin too!'

# CHAPTER XXV

## AT THE PIANO

I FOLLOW Mrs. Westby's pale blue gown into
the drawing-room in extremely low spirits.
The dinner hour has not been a jovial one,
and now I am in for a snubbing ; I can see it
in every feature of Lady Dromore's face, and
in every curve of Mrs. Westby's figure as she
waddles in front of me.

Great Heavens ! How justly the poet
might have exclaimed—

. . . . I hate a dumpy woman !

if he had known Mrs. Westby!

So I pull myself together as best I may,
hold my head in the air and stiffen my weary
knees. If Lady Dromore is very rude, I shall
inquire minutely after that sister of hers who,

she declares, is travelling in America, but who is really in a dipsomaniac establishment near Dorking, as I accidentally discovered the other day.

Matters do not reach this extremity, however. The snubbing is more passive than active, and consists mainly in Lady Dromore and Mrs. Westby utterly ignoring my existence, while at the same time they evince a delicate sixth sense of the presence of an outsider by the dignity with which they confine their conversation to indifferent topics.

I warm my feet carefully at the fire; then, finding that occupation pall in time, I stroll slowly across the room to the open piano and begin one of Chopin's dreamiest nocturnes.

Mrs. Stuart and Frances have gone into the little conservatory that opens out of the drawing-room. From where I sit I can see them in earnest conversation among the chrysanthemums. Frances is twisting the creamy petals of a jagged Meg Merrilies in her fidgety fingers ; but they are not talking about the flowers, I am sure. Never did Frances pour out so voluble a stream of words over the merits of any queen among them all—rose, lily, or chrysanthemum ; some very personal interest is lighting up her face, and now she lets the Meg Merrilies fly back on its long stem, and lays her hand affectionately on Mrs. Stuart's arm.

One by one the men drop in, and bestow their persons where it seemeth good unto them. Mr. Mostyn is struggling with a yawn, and undisguisedly looking at his watch. Bryan, with unconscious heroism, makes straight for Lady Dromore and Mrs. Westby, but how long it takes to convince him that he might as well have attempted to storm the Redan single-handed I cannot tell, for Sir Allan has paused by the piano, and looks down hesitatingly at me.

It is pity that is softening his face—I know each line of it so well ; but even his pity I

E 2

will not scorn. Almost superstitiously do I
long to be on friendly terms with him; it
seems to me as if I could bear my lot more
easily and do my duty more steadily after one
kind word from Allan.

'How has your musical education been
getting on?' I ask hurriedly, smothering
Chopin's sighs with remorseless hand so that
they may accompany me monotonously pia-
nissimo. 'Do you know "God save the
Queen" now when you hear it?'

'Not unless I see fellows taking off their
hats,' with a reluctant smile.

'At any rate you are spared a good deal,'
I continue, not caring much what I talk about
so long as I keep him there. If he would
only pull up that little cane chair and sit
down! 'You would listen quite gaily to a
first lesson on the violin, I suppose?'

'Just as gaily as I should listen to Joa-
chim,' he answers, laughing outright. His
hand is on the back of the chair now.

'Did you write that article in the "Tri-Weekly," on Colonies in England?' I ask with sudden boldness.

Allan looks sharply at me and frowns. 'What put that into your head?'

'Part of it reminded me so forcibly of some of our old talks that I felt sure you wrote it,' I answer. 'Sit down and tell me if you think of trying that experiment about a self-supporting village in the north.'

He pulls up the chair and sits down, but 'I am not going to talk about my colony to you,' he says calmly. 'I used to imagine at one time that you were capable of taking an interest in such things, but I have had my eyes opened since then.'

'I don't know what you mean; I never set up for being any better than other girls. You always knew I was fond of amusing myself, and—and——' I am so anxious to regain his good opinion, or rather to discover why I have forfeited it, that my breath comes short, and my wits take to themselves wings and fly away.

'At any rate,' I exclaim desperately, throwing all defence of my character to the winds, 'I am no different now from what I used to be, except that trouble has sobered me ; and we used to be very good friends. Why can't we be friends again ? '

Allan meets my wistful look with a puzzled expression.

'No, I dare say you are the same, but I had a different idea of you.' Then, with a sudden flash of wrath, 'I cannot understand how you could do such a cold-blooded, heartless thing ! '

What does he mean? Is it my marriage he is alluding to? He knows that I only married Bryan after he had deserted me, and it is horribly unfair of him to talk of heartlessness.

Open-eyed and breathless with excitement, we are gazing at one another, Allan leaning forward with tilted chair, I turning round on the music stool.

'I don't understand you,' I answer slowly. ' How could you possibly expect me——' and I pause, searching for words to remind him of the past, and yet which will not be disloyal to Bryan.

Allan waits with painful intentness.

'How could any girl be expected——' I begin again, when a light laugh rings out behind us, and Frances' hand is laid on my shoulder.

'At any rate *I* am not afraid of her,' she says. 'Mrs. Stuart wants you to play again, Esmé, but she does not like to ask you. She says you made such crushing remarks the other day about objecting to accompany conversation.'

'So I do generally,' I exclaim, trembling with disappointment and turning round in piteous appeal to Frances. Oh, how cruel of her to rob me of my one chance! ' But I am in a more modest frame of mind this evening, and I will play the most encouraging of accompaniments if you will go and mollify Mrs. Stuart.'

'Very well,' says Frances, without budging an inch. 'Only don't play Chopin; he is too depressing. Play that thing Bryan is so fond of; you know what I mean—that waltz he always asks you for, every evening after dinner. She ought to be in good practice, Sir Allan; she plays to Bryan by the hour together!'

At this soothing picture of domestic bliss Allan starts up hastily and looks around for a retreat. By a deft movement Frances places herself in front of him, so that they walk away from the piano together with the decorous appearance of lady first, gentleman following.

'I can assure you there are moments when I find myself forcibly reminded that "two is company, three is trumpery,"' says Frances, smiling back at Allan over her shoulder, as she moves towards a vacant corner. 'Bryan is so devoted, and Esmé is one of those affectionate people——'

Her voice dies off to a confidential murmur, and I turn back to the piano to hide my mortification as best I may under a volley of notes.

'Si oiseau j'étais, à toi je volerais!' I dare say; but what sort of a reception should I get?

As I rattle lightly along something in the very contrast of the music brings Mendelssohn's beautiful setting of the 55th Psalm to my mind—

Oh for the wings of a dove! Far away, far away
would I roam,

and the tears fill my eyes. There is no rest, no peace for me. I am full of trouble, and the thought that it is partly my own doing makes it no easier to bear.

There is dead silence for a moment as I finish. The light brilliance of the bird-like rush has caught people's attention, although of course they are not so impressed as they would have been with a good musical box.

'Wonderful execution!' says Mr. Westby.

'You must practise a great deal, Mrs. Mansfield,' remarks Lord Dromore, with the air of a critic.

'That's the curious part of it,' interposes Bryan, coming up to my side; 'she scarcely practises at all.' And he rubs his hands with modest triumph.

Lady Dromore now considers it high time to divert attention from so unworthy an object.

'We must be going,' she declares, retrieving her lord with a stony glance, and marching up to our hostess to say good-bye.

'No, wait a minute,' whispers Mrs. Stuart, when I too would take my leave. 'I want to speak to you. Good-bye, Mr. Mostyn.'

Then putting her hand through my arm and guiding me through the drawing-room, 'Come and show me which chrysanthemums you would like cuttings of,' she begins loudly ; and I wonder within myself what she can be driving at, for never have I breathed a word about chrysanthemums to her.

When we are fairly inside the conservatory, 'I want you to lend me Frances,' she says persuasively ; 'she would like to come and stay with me if you have no objection.'

'Of course I have no objection,' I return, rather puzzled, nevertheless, at this sudden friendship. We have known Mrs. Stuart all our lives, but have never stayed at one another's houses before.

'Do you want her to come to you before Christmas or after?'

'Christmas! Dear Esmé, how innocent you are! Why, I want her to come to me to-morrow. Sir Allan is only staying a few days longer.'

'To-morrow!'

The blood rushes in an angry wave to my face. So that is what she and Frances were talking about in here after dinner! Frances must have given her a good broad hint that she would like to come. How indecent she can be! It really is not kind of Mrs. Stuart to encourage her in such a barefaced husband-hunt.

'Yes, to-morrow. You don't mind, do you?'

And Mrs. Stuart looks up curiously at me. Something in her expression warns me to be on my guard. How far have Frances' confidences led her, I wonder?

'I do not mind,' I answer slowly, 'except that it seems rather queer for her to come over so suddenly.'

'No one will notice it,' returns Mrs. Stuart. 'There are no women in the house, and men never see anything.'

'N—no,' I murmur dubiously.

'It is a pity to lose the opportunity,' she goes on. 'It would be such a splendid match for Frances. He really does seem taken with her, and if he leaves us without proposing she won't have much chance. All the girls in England will be at his heels, and a man so soon gets spoilt!'

'You are very interested in the affair,' I say vaguely, as she pauses. I must say something, and it certainly must not be what I think.

'Of course I am! Allan Vaudrey is one of my best friends, and if he marries a stranger I shall never see anything more of him. Now I always have liked Frances.'

'Yes,' I murmur, with parroty assent; 'most people do like Frances.'

Something in my stiff, unsympathetic bearing annoys Mrs. Stuart.

'I think also,' she exclaims, in a tone I have never heard from her before, and with an impatient shrug of the shoulders, 'that women who have married happily and well ought to do all that is in their power for girls —particularly for a nice girl in Frances' lonely and desolate position!'

Clearly I must look to my fair fame and beware of slander. So, repressing the angry retort that rises to my lips, and wreathing them instead in a very tolerable smile, I rejoin good-humouredly, 'Of course we ought! Only please don't call Frances lonely or desolate. My home is always hers; and as to paying

visits to-morrow or at any time, she is perfectly free to make her own plans. Shall we
go back to the drawing-room now? It is
getting late.'

A more approving consent I cannot bring
myself to give; but apparently, like Mercutio's
wound, 'it is enough,' for Mrs. Stuart calls
out gaily as we emerge from the conservatory—

'Frances, you must be a good, obedient
girl, and come over here to-morrow. Esmé
says she can spare you better now than later
on, and I was really beginning to think that
your long-talked-of visit would never come
off.'

# CHAPTER XXVI

## CHARITIES

FRANCES wastes no words during the long drive home; having attained her object she leans back in satisfied silence.

Bryan also is satisfied; though wherefore it would be hard to say, the slight facts he alludes to affording but insufficient ground, to an impartial mind, for rejoicing over his social success. Lady Dromore, it seems, grunted twice in answer to his conversational attempts; Mrs. Westby informed him that Prince Henry of Battenberg was coming to breakfast the next time the hounds met at Rakefield, and that she had invited all the *nice* people she knew to meet his Royal Highness; and Lord Dromore quite agreed when he—Bryan—remarked that it was a cold evening.

All that night I lie awake, open-eyed,
pondering many things.

At first bitter wrath stirs my blood and I
toss angrily about, cursing my own hasty folly
in for ever putting a gulf between my love
and me, and chafing against the unkind fate
which seems determined that we shall not
even be friends.

As for Frances and her contemptible tricks
and wiles, I will tolerate them no longer. I
will give her plainly to understand that if she
wishes to remain under my roof she must alter
her behaviour. I have enough to worry me
surely, without needlessly enduring her pin-
pricks.

But as the still hours wear on a wiser calm
steals over me. Joy and happiness, it is true,
I have put away from me for ever ; but peace
may at least be mine—the repose that comes
from perseverance in well-doing. I have tried
hard to do right lately ; yet peace and I have
been far from each other. Rather, indeed,

have I learnt how much one can endure and
still present a smiling face to the world.  How
am I to earn it?  Only by doing God's will,
the will divinely summed up in those mighty
words, 'Thou shalt love the Lord thy God
. . . and thy neighbour as thyself.'

The first commandment is for my heart
and me.  The second . . . how am I fulfill-
ing it?

I told Bryan plainly before I married him
that there could be no pretence of affection
on my part, but that I would do my duty to
him to the utmost of my power; and I am
keeping my word.  Never once have I flinched
from his side, and never once have I spoken
to him with deliberate unkindness; to be
candid with myself, I must confess to occa-
sional snaps and sharp answers, but they have
been always quickly repented of and promptly
repaired.  Surely if my cheek is constantly
burning with mortification at his sayings, and
my eyes often lowered in annoyance at his

doings, that is my punishment, not my crime.

With regard to Frances my conscience is not so clear. What right have I to be annoyed at her flirtation with Allan Vaudrey?

Yes, I dare say it is inconsiderate, unkind, unsisterly of her to single out the very man whom I have so loved and for whom I have so suffered. But why should I interfere if such a desirable marriage be possible for her?

For Allan's sake?

In spite of his unworthy treatment of me, I still think him immeasurably too good for Frances; but if she pleases him what business is that of mine? Though he married a paragon universally admitted to combine in her one person all the graces and all the virtues. *I* should certainly consider her a most objec - tionable creature! Frances is no worse than other girls, I suppose (I have never had an exalted opinion of my own sex); she is bright, pretty, good-tempered, and, with plenty of money to give her what she wants, is a charming creature to live with. In the old days—ah! those happy old days!—I used always to think her a delightful girl; and if adversity has brought out certain bad qualities, the happy sun of prosperity will perhaps warm her back to her own genial self again.

So what need have I, for Sir Allan Vaudrey's sake, to throw obstacles in the way of my sister's meeting him?

I had better acknowledge the truth. It is jealousy that is disturbing me so—jealousy patent to others—to Mrs. Stuart and to Frances—though I will scarce admit it myself.

To know one's weakness is half the battle; and I rise in the morning, pale and weary, but determined to do my duty.

Frances eyes me apprehensively when we

meet at the breakfast-table, evidently thinking
it possible that at the eleventh hour I may
try and prevent her visit.

'Will you have the victoria or the
brougham this afternoon?' I ask, smiling at
her with the teapot poised in mid air. 'I am
going to ride, so it won't make any difference
to me which you prefer.'

'Then I will have the brougham,' she says
with a little sigh of relief, the red colour
fluttering back to her face—Frances' complexion is as delicately variable as a child's.
'I need not leave here till four, so as to get
there about tea-time. That's the most propi-
tious moment to arrive, isn't it?'

'Yes, I think so,' I agree—a twinge shooting through me as I picture the group round
Mrs. Stuart's tea-table. 'I have told Julie to
see to your packing, and to take you anything
of mine that you would care to wear. You
would like my pink ostrich fan to go with
your pink gown, wouldn't you?'

Frances shakes her head with a serious air.

'I shall not take my pink gown,' she says solemnly. 'I am only going to wear my old white ones. Simplicity and modest merit are the watchwords of this crisis.'

The candid exposition of her plans is here stopped by the arrival of Bryan upon the scene. He has not until now grasped the fact that Frances is going to leave us for a while ; and his joy upon being informed of her approaching departure is indecently manifest.

' Stay as long as you feel inclined,' he urges repeatedly. ' We shall be very glad to return any kindness the Stuarts show you. I can make it up to Stuart over the shooting; he shall have a good place when we shoot the Home Covert.'

.    .    .    .    .

Now that Frances, with nods and becks and many a smile, is fairly off, I determine to take advantage of my *tête-à-tête* with Bryan

to get a clearer idea of our monetary
position.

I am not at all satisfied with the arrangement of our finances. Bryan encourages me
to run up endless bills and give reckless
orders, but I never can get any money from
him ; nor has he ever given me a clear statement of his means, often as I have asked him.
Although our establishment is mounted upon
an extravagant scale, and the expenditure in
the stables and out of doors generally is lavish,
twenty thousand a year is a large income, and
will, I dare say, cover everything when once
the cost of furnishing is cleared off. But I
want to hear definitely from Bryan that we
are justified in spending that amount ; and I
should like an allowance for my own private
use, that I might economise upon my clothes
and have some money for charity.

Bryan is so touchy and queer about his
affairs, that I select the moment for my inves-
tigations with care. After dinner he is always

sleepy, and if disturbed, inclined to be frac-
tious; after breakfast, when we are not hunting,
he retires to the library and writes mysterious
documents which he shuffles away when I go
in; but after luncheon he is generally in a
bland, chatty frame of mind.

'Bryan, I have not been at all pleased
with Mrs. Marston lately,' I begin, one day
about half-past two. My choice of opening
subject has also been well considered; Mrs.
Marston is the housekeeper, and Bryan usually
loves talking about the servants.

'Haven't you, though? What has she
been doing?'

'I can't get proper accounts from her;
and it's a regular case of "pull devil, pull
baker" when I want to look at the tradespeople's books.'

'Is that all?' returns Bryan. 'She has
evidently lived in families where these things
are considered beneath the lady's notice.'

'Very likely; but they are not beneath

the lady's notice in this family. And that reminds me—how much do you think we ought to spend in the house, Bryan ? '

' To spend in the house ! ' repeats my husband vacantly. ' I really don't know. Oh, I see here that the Duke of Sackville is not expected to recover.'

He is leaning over the billiard-table, drinking in news from the imaginative columns of a Society paper.

' Poor fellow ! ' I respond philosophically. ' But you must have some idea of our income Bryan ? If you would only just tell me how much we ought to spend, I could arrange everything accordingly.'

' I don't see that any fresh arrangement is wanted,' with a sulky shake of ' The Scavenger.' ' It is no use my going into figures with you ; women never understand business. When I complain of the amount of money spent, it will be time enough for you to talk about fresh arrangements.'

'I know I don't understand business,' endeavouring to combine meekness and firmness in happy proportions; 'no one can be more ignorant of it than I. But you might explain to me how much money you have and what it brings you in every year. You surely don't mind my knowing, do you, Bryan?'

'I don't think you display much confidence in me when you bother me so about details,' answers Bryan, evasively important.

I sigh impatiently and am mute.

'You have everything you want, have you not?' he pursues, gathering up his paper and preparing for retreat.

'I have, in one way,' I answer slowly; 'but I should like some money for charity. I never have a penny to give away.'

'To give away!' repeats Bryan with an astonished air; 'and you have just been grumbling about expense! How inconsistent women are, to be sure!'

Then in a softer tone—for Bryan does

not like to refuse me anything—he asks,
' Well! How much do you want? Five
pounds? Ten pounds? Look here, now, I'll
give you all the ready money I have about
me.'

And he empties his pockets on the billiard-
table.

' Six pounds and eight shillings. There,
you can make ducks and drakes of that! I
don't know what you will be able to do with
it, as the neighbourhood is by no means a
poor one. Well, ta-ta, I must go and see
Godbold about those new forcing-pits.'

Wherewith he marches off quite alertly for
him ; and I, like the damsel in the song, am
left lamenting.

Next day, however, a new aspect of the
case has occurred to Bryan.

' By the way, Esmé,' he says, emerging
from the library with his hands full of papers,
' I find there is a good deal of sense in what
you were saying yesterday as to giving money

away. I have been looking up these applica-
tions, and I see that the best people about here
give very regularly. Lord Dromore, for
instance, is an annual subscriber to this lot,'
holding up the right-hand packet, 'and has
given donations to these,' flourishing the left.
' You see,' apologetically, ' I have never lived
in the country before, and it did not strike me
how such things would be criticised. You
were quite right to speak about it—quite
right.'

I open my mouth to deprecate this un-
merited praise, but shut it again feebly ; an
explanation with Bryan is so exhausting.

' I wonder it never occurred to Frances to
remind me of the importance of well-chosen
almsgiving before,' continues my husband,
the irritated expression appearing in his face
which Frances' name always brings there.
' She is generally quick enough to mention
anything bearing upon our social position.'

' What are these charities ? ' I ask, slipping

off the elastic bands with which he has secured the two bundles.

' Don't mix them, dear,' exclaims Bryan hastily. ' I thought I could not do better than follow Lord Dromore's lead, so I have sorted out his subscriptions and his donations. I shall write cheques for the same amounts.'

# CHAPTER XXVII

## THE BALL

FRANCES betook herself to Mrs. Stuart's on a Thursday.

The following Monday Bryan goes out hunting alone. By artful manipulation of that feminine weapon, a bad headache, I have persuaded him to leave me at home in peace —a peace untarnished by fear of any interruption whatsoever, as I emphasise my holiday by giving prompt orders that no visitors are to be admitted.

Then, flinging aside all pretence of occupation, I indulge in the doubtful luxury of my own thoughts.

From room to room I wander, drawing long breaths of relief at my unwonted liberty.

For one whole day I am free to sigh or to smile, to laugh or to cry, as the fancy takes me, without the necessity of a full and radical explanation of what has pleased or grieved me. For one whole day I am released from Frances' inquisitive and too-comprehending gaze, from Bryan's interminable discussion of the dullest details. Poor Bryan! Had ever man so heavy a conversational touch, so fatal a habit of worrying a subject to death?

This morning he prosed steadily through breakfast about the grilled chicken in front of him. I wonder, should I think Allan Vaudrey dull if he talked about grilled chicken? Rather, I am afraid, should I consider his remarks worthy of being printed as a companion essay to Elia's 'Roast Pig!'

It is very hard that my interest in Allan should so terribly have outlived his interest in me. I am the same Esmé, whose every movement his eyes used to follow; yet how terribly is my influence over him gone!

I walk to the long glass at the end of the drawing-room and inspect my charms critically in the cold grey November light.

No, it is no waning in my beauty that has estranged him. Though I have grown very thin, I am prettier than ever, and, as I stand gazing into those soft dark eyes as though they were a stranger's, a great flood of self-pity comes over me. I look so young, so fragile, to be so hopeless—and in despair I cast myself down on a sofa hard by and burst into bitter tears.

I must have lain there, prone and sobbing, for a full quarter of an hour, when a discreet cough breaks upon my ear.

Burrowing, face downwards, between two cushions is doubtless not apt to quicken one's sense of hearing; still I think if Dixon had rattled the door-handle, or tripped over a convenient footstool, he might have aroused me, instead of coming within three feet before he gives the faintest warning of his presence.

'Miss Nugent is at the door, ma'am,' he begins composedly, as I raise myself with a jerk, and present the back of my head perpendicularly instead of horizontally for his minute inspection ; ' she is on horseback, and would be much obliged if you would come out and speak to her, as she does not wish to dismount.'

' Who is with Miss Nugent ? ' I ask, in hideous perturbation, as I bethink me of my red nose and swollen eyelids.

' Miss Nugent is alone, ma'am.'

' Go and say that I will come to her in a moment.'

Which moment is spent in mopping my eyes and pushing back my ruffled hair. How can I ever be sufficiently thankful that the gods have inspired Frances to ride over alone ? What should I have done if any one else had arrived to find me in such obvious woe for no obvious reason ? It is bad enough to have to meet my sister's cool eyes out of

doors in the broad light, and this will be a
lesson to me to bottle up my tears in future
for the privacy of my chamber and nightfall.
Languidly I cross the hall.   What can Frances
want, I wonder ?   Some more gowns perhaps;
I thought she was taking too few.   Dixon
throws open the front door and I emerge upon
the big stone step, bareheaded and defence-
less from the garish day, to find not only
Frances but Sir Allan Vaudrey waiting for
me.   It is too late to draw back, but I cannot
control the startled exclamation—

'Dixon told me you were alone, Frances!'

'Yes.   Don't be angry with him, poor
fellow!' with a sunny smile, well aimed over
my shoulder at the mendacious domestic.   'I
told him to say so because I didn't want the
bother of getting off, and I was afraid you
might decline to interview any one else upon
the doorstep.   So we agreed that Sir Allan
did not count!'

.   She is mounted upon a fidgety grey cob

and looks almost like a child, with her tiny waist and slim shoulders. All Frances' height is in her legs. Sir Allan, on a bay weight-carrier, is well behind her, and as he confines his greeting to a bow and a brief 'Good-morning,' has very much the air of squire in attendance. But alas! I know from old experience that those grey eyes of his are far-seeing and astute, and I much fear that the poor little stratagem of shading my forehead from the light with outstretched fingers will be of small avail in concealing such palpable tear-stains. Surely never was burst of weeping more ill-timed!

'Well, you don't seem overjoyed at beholding us,' pursues my sister, as she restrains her steed from a playful attempt to nibble my gown; 'and yet we have come a good bit out of our way to see you. Bryan told us we should find you at home.'

'Oh, you have seen Bryan, have you?' is all I can manage to get out.

'We have had that honour. What a shame of him to leave you behind, you poor old darling! It is such a jolly morning!' in compassionate accents.

'How absurd you are, Frances! As if Bryan would leave me at home if I wanted to go!' I exclaim angrily.

'Oh, of course I know he is perfect,' smiling provokingly. 'But I haven't lost the chance of a run to-day to hear you sing the praises of your beloved. I came to say that Mrs. Stuart has asked me to stay till next week and go to the Brackham ball with her. You don't mind, do you?'

'Not at all.'

'And then I thought that you need not turn out unless you like,' pursues Frances. 'I know you were going principally on my account.'

'Thank you,' I reply shortly.

I think Allan might say something to me instead of sitting there in grim, observant silence. He is evidently going to stay for the ball.

'We must be jogging now,' says Frances, with calm appropriation of her escort. 'You are sure you don't mind my staying on? No? I thought you wouldn't. I expect you and Bryan are perfectly delighted to get rid of me. I suppose you are

Still amorous and fond and billing,
Like Philip and Mary on a shilling.

Eh?'

'If you have nothing more to say, I think I will go in,' I remark, loftily ignoring her odious little couplet. 'It is very cold standing here. Good-morning, Sir Allan. Good-bye, Frances.'

And I march indoors, with as much dignity as the circumstances will allow. From behind the morning-room window-curtains I watch them ride off, Frances very close to Sir Allan's knee, and her pretty chin tilted up in the air towards him as she chatters away confidingly.

I expect she is observing that dear Esmé must have had a tiff with her husband, as nothing else ever makes her cry; and that it is a most unusual occurrence, for a more devoted couple could not be found in the length and breadth of our island than Bryan Mansfield and her sister!

I abandon myself to no more tears after this; not that the cause for them is less, but that wrath has momentarily swallowed up woe, and my anger is all-absorbing and inclusive. I am furious with Frances, furious also with Sir Allan, though what the poor man has done except hold his tongue it would be hard to say; and most furious with myself for the undignified figure I have cut this morning. To be found sobbing noisily by the butler is annoying; but to have my blurred and distorted face mercilessly exposed to the prolonged gaze of the man before whom I would fain wear my fairest appearance is hard indeed. What a foil I must have presented to Frances'

dainty skin and clear-cut features! Of course
I ought not to care so terribly about Sir Allan's
thoughts of me; I know that perfectly well;
and the struggle to push him out of my mind
alternates cheerfully during the rest of the
day with wrathful invectives against Fate and
hopeless attempts at a more righteous frame
of mind.

.     .     .     .     .

'You look well turned out, Esmé,' says
Bryan, as he surveys me critically before
we start for the Brackham ball; 'but you
are very pale. Can't you do anything for
it, eh?'

'Do anything for it?' I repeat inquiringly.
'How do you mean?'

'Couldn't you touch up your cheeks a
little?' he explains. 'I dare say there is
some rouge about,' and he peers among the
silver bottles and nicknacks of my toilet-
table.

'Non, Monsieur, Madame n'en a pas; mais

moi je puis en trouver,' shrieks Julie, flying
delightedly in the direction of her own apart-
ment.

'Come back, Julie, at once,' I vociferate,
'and fasten my mantle. Mr. Mansfield was
only joking. He knows I would not paint my
face. Now, Bryan, shall we start?'

'I don't know why you shouldn't paint
your face,' grumbles my husband, two minutes
later, as we bowl along in the cosy little
brougham. 'You will have to begin some
time or other, and the least touch of rouge
would have been an immense improvement
to-night. You have been looking very white
lately.'

'It is the cold weather,' I answer cheerfully. 'You have no idea how red I shall get
as soon as I begin to dance; a peony will be
faded compared with my complexion.'

'Have you been feeling the cold so much?'
asks Bryan anxiously. 'You have never
mentioned it before. Would you like to go

abroad after Christmas? I think I will get
Dr. Singleton to see you to-morrow.'

'Nonsense, Bryan!' I exclaim, laughing
in spite of myself at the idea of the village
doctor making a palpable examination of my
heart as a cure for its impalpable woes. 'I
am perfectly well. How hard the roads
sound! Do you think there will be any hunting to-morrow?'

I am being borne along to the ball in a
tolerably jovial frame of mind, all things considered. Hope is hard to kill; and one has
better chances of a *tête-à-tête* at a ball than at
any other festivity. Allan can hardly fail to
ask me to dance; and though it be only once
we shall be practically alone for a quarter of
an hour, in which not even Frances can interrupt us. Nor does any fear of feminine snubs
assail my mind. At a ball, as in a better
world, I shall rise superior to dowagers.
What matter the frowns and averted glances
of whole bench-loads of old women when

there are plenty of men to make a fuss over me? So with radiant mien, not wholly feigned, I enter the well-known room.

The dowagers are there—as uninteresting a dado as heart of man could conceive; the men are there—in five minutes I am surrounded by a mob of black and red hunt coats; and Allan is there, not dancing, but standing drearily by a door, and looking supremely out of tune with the whole festivity.

With much forethought I have decided that I will give him three dances, if he ask for them at once; two, if he delay a little; and one only, if he be conspicuously slack in coming forward. It has scarcely entered into my calculations that he should not come forward at all; and yet that apparently is the course he has chalked out for himself. He sees me clearly enough, and with cool politeness returns the bow I bestow upon him as our eyes meet. Now, for a woman to look away from the men who are thronging around her in a ball-room and bow to an individual who shows no intention whatever of joining the throng, is already a tolerable advance on her part. I can do no more.

Blankly I abandon every dance but one to those who clamour most eagerly; it is too obvious I need not retain two, much less three. Tum-te-tum, tum-te-tum, goes the band, and off we start in ridiculous accord. Is there another form of mortal amusement so degradingly foolish as a dance? To think of human beings who ought to have some work to do in the world (and who, if they have not, are of all men most miserable) twirling round in the middle of the night, mostly with tired, aching bodies, to the monotonous, purposeless, mechanical twanging of instruments! It is true I did not take so bitter a view of dancing ten minutes ago, before Allan Vaudrey surveyed me indifferently and coolly from the opposite side of the room; but while I am being whisked around in Lord Chadwyck's arms, my dress getting torn and my elbows scratched, it is powerfully borne in upon me that within the last twelve months I have grown too old for a ball-room.

My discovery, fortunately for me, does not affect my popularity. I may be tongue-tied and absent-minded, but what matters that at a ball? The poetic eloquence of Sappho and the wit of Aspasia would be superfluous and unmarketable commodities with dancing men; all they ask is a slim waist to put their respective arms around, a smart gown to walk with, and a person inside the gown who can keep step with their varied eccentricities of motion.

These requirements properly fulfilled, no further strain upon the intellect is necessary to satisfy them. So I scamper wildly with Lord Chadwyck, turn slowly under the gaselier in the centre of the room with Major Johnstone, take hurried little rushes with Mr. Mostyn, and blockade the ring of revolving

couples with Archie Sinclair; while the self-
same smile does duty when Lord Chadwyck
says the room is getting hot, when Major
Johnstone tells me his grandmother is dead
and has left him a pot of money, when Mr.
Mostyn remarks that he rode a brute to-day
who came down with him twice, and when
Archie Sinclair audaciously inquires whether
my new aunt has converted Uncle Frank yet.

Meanwhile Sir Allan stands about the room
and dances with no one.

# CHAPTER XXVIII

## THE CORRIDOR

BRYAN, on the contrary, is dancing energetically, and presenting a living illustration of
the maxim, ' If you cannot get what you like,
it is best to like what you can get.' Meeting
with no success when he invites the young and
fair to join the mazy dance with him, he philosophically falls back upon the elderly and
ugly. The higher the damsel's rank, the older
and uglier may she be. He has drawn the
line at Janet Harding, the Brackham curate's
daughter, who, verging upon forty, smiles
liberally upon *anything* in masculine attire ;
but he is more than content to be seen marching about with Lady Margaret Fitzduc, of
years, wrinkles, and frightfulness untold. He

has taken seven ladies down to supper, and finds himself more cordially received at this crisis of the evening than at any other time.

'Awful sell for Jack being left out in the cold,' says Major Johnstone, still upon the theme of his grandmother and her ducats; 'but he has really been going on too absurdly. Did you hear of his swarming up a lamp post in Pall Mall with two policemen's helmets under his arms?'

'What for?' I inquire absently.

'For a lark, of course. He stopped the bobbies one after the other, and told 'em he was an M.P. just going to introduce a new bill for the reformation of the police headgear, and that he wanted to examine the width of their brims. Then off he bolted. I came along a few minutes afterwards and found him astride upon the lamp-post, reading out extracts from the " Police Manual for the guidance of constables in unusual circumstances."'

'What did you do?' I ask, with provoking inattention. Frances is talking eagerly to Bryan, to my great astonishment, and with a smile and a turn of the head which I certainly have not seen her practise upon him since the Riverdalian days.

'Do? Nothing, of course,' responds Major Johnstone with an aggrieved air. His little story has fallen so very flat.

'At any rate, I hope it was not you who informed the grandmother,' I remark lightly. 'Come and talk to my sister. I have not spoken to her yet.'

But by the time we reach Frances, Bryan has left her, darting off with most unusual alacrity. I feel inclined to dart after him in my morbid suspicion of Frances' prompting, but it takes some time to change the current of Major Johnstone's ideas, and he has only just mastered the fact that I want to speak to my sister.

'How are you, dear?' she says, meeting

me more than half-way, and laying an unusually caressing hand upon my arm. 'You
look so nice, and your gown is quite the
prettiest in the room.'

'Thank you. I can bear that honour
calmly.'

'I dare say,' acquiesces Frances with a
laugh. 'The British provincial female has
outdone herself to-night. Well, are you glad
to hear that I am coming back to-morrow?'

'Very,' I answer with unfeigned relief.
Sir Allan has not been paying her the least
attention to-night, and when she comes home,
and he leaves Mrs. Stuart's, surely she will
turn her beguiling elsewhere, and I shall have
my torture relaxed. Any other man with
money would do just as well for Frances. By
the way, Major Johnstone must be very rich
now; he was well off before, and old Lady
Killock's money has, after the manner of
money, come where it was least wanted.

Why should not Frances try her hand upon him?

'Will you stay with my sister, Major Johnstone? I see my husband looking wildly round for some one—he wants me, I suspect.'

I am slipping quietly off when Frances catches my hand detainingly.

'No, no, it is not you Bryan is looking for —it is some one else. Tell me, what time can you send for me to-morrow?' And before she releases me my next partner comes up.

.      .      .      .      .

I wonder if any married woman in love with another man than her husband ever felt herself so painfully degraded by it as I. As I walk and dance around that square, unbedecked ball-room, my knees trembling beneath me with agitation, my nerves on the stretch with excitement, it seems to me as if my humiliation must be written upon my face; as if everyone who passed me must be able to read there how horribly I love Allan

Vaudrey. To add to my misery, I am conscious that I should not be so ashamed if Allan cared for me as I for him; but to have this sick longing for the touch, the sound of the voice of a man who has dismissed me from his mind with such ease, is mortifying as well as wicked. And alas! a mind must be more perfectly attuned to the heavenly harmonies than mine not to be as much troubled by the mortification as the wickedness.

My partner is discoursing with bland unconsciousness in my ear. To most of the misery in this world there seems to be a babbling accompaniment of small talk; the respectable, recognised sorrows which admit of open tears and undisguised mourning may be summed up on the fingers of one's hand. Surely they cannot be so hard to bear. If I could live in a black gown and sob noisily and openly all day long, I believe it would go half way towards curing me of my woes.

'Yes ; and it was a mangy vixen after all,' finishes Mr. Mostyn dismally.

'How tiresome!' I respond. 'Then she didn't give you any run ? '

'Just crept up Birch Hill like a snail ! '

Sir Allan has returned to the doorway through which Bryan disappeared a few minutes ago, and is looking inquiringly round the room. What lucky fair one is he searching for? Not Frances ; his eye alights on her and passes her over. He is coming my way at last! Allah be praised ! How glad I am and how undignified to be so glad !

'They'll catch it from anything,' continues Mr. Mostyn. 'I have known a toy terrier start the mange in a whole country-side——'

'Is it too late to ask for a dance, Mrs. Mansfield?' asks Allan.

'I think I have one left.'

I hope that careless accent was not over-done. Mr. Mostyn evidently does not notice anything, for he tucks my hand under his arm

again in his jerky fashion, and resumes the
even tenor of our way, and his disquisition
upon the iniquitous diseases of the vulpine
race. Foxes alone agitate his heart.

Half an hour later Allan and I are seated
together on one of the few benches in the
corridor outside the ball-room.

The corridor has been reclaimed from the
air of heaven and the frosts of earth by the
aid of a little match-boarding and much bunt-
ing. Winds icier than an Arctic blast sport
playfully with the tendrils of my hair and pene-
trate gaily down my bare back ; but though
each breezelet brought me certain bronchitis,
and each draught lifelong rheumatism, I
would hail them with cheerful indifference,
for have I not at last got Allan all to myself,
with no Frances to interrupt, and no Bryan to
irritate ?

Conversation at first hangs fire. Small
wonder. Does not Heine tell us that when he
first met Goethe, after a weary pilgrimage to

behold the features of the Godlike being whom
he had long reverenced from afar, no more
exalted remark occurred to him wherewith to
initiate the feast of reason and the flow of soul
so eagerly anticipated during many a long
winter night, than that ' the plums along the
roadside from Jena to Weimar were excellent ? '

If such paralysis of the wits thus assailed
the brilliant poet, surely two ordinary mortals
like Allan and myself may be forgiven for
finding nothing more sympathetic to begin
with than—

'I am afraid you are rather in a draught,'
and—

'Not at all, thanks. I like fresh air, you
know.'

Then after a pause—

'I see you are as fond of dancing as ever,'
says Allan.

'I am not fond of it at all,' I retort hastily.

' Appearances are deceitful, then.'

' Very likely. I don't know how the world would go on wagging if we all looked and did as we felt inclined.'

' It is very easy to some people to conceal their feelings,' says Allan bitterly.

Now Allan has a nice voice, and in speaking to women it is soft and deferential; only to me it has lately been hard and sharp. When I consider this in calm solitude I comfort myself by arguing that the exception betrays strong feeling of some kind, and that after all I would rather he addressed me in different tones—harsh though they be—from those in which he agrees with Mrs. Westby that it is a fine day; but at the time the unaccustomed voice jars upon me, and makes me shrink within myself. Another pause.

' Did you like India?' I ask desperately. I must say something, and the minutes are slipping on.

' Very much. I had such a cheerful time there, and I heard such delightful news.'

' What news ? '

' Of a wedding.'

' Ah ! That is the first time I have heard a wedding spoken of with approbation. They are usually considered gruesome things.'

' I did not mean to speak of this wedding with approbation. I quite agree with you that it was a gruesome thing.'

' Really? where did it take place? in England or in India ? '

' In England.'

' Then I should have thought you would have heard of it with complete indifference. I imagine you are one of those happy beings whose friends when out of sight are out of mind.'

' Thank you.'

I steal a side-glance at him. He looks very cross ; and the conversation is not taking the turn I intended. Inside the ball-room the violins are getting excited ; the waltz is more than half-way through.  Allan shall start the next remark anyhow, and I will remain motionless and speechless until he says something.

As I make this doughty resolve I open my fan with a would-be careless flourish ; but to my horror I see it shaking violently as if held in a palsied hand.  I hastily shut it up again, and clasp my hands firmly together under its feathers, so that trembling fingers may not betray me.  Then I look cautiously around to see if Allan has noticed my discomposure, and meet his eyes bent full upon me with an anxious, searching expression whence all crossness has vanished.

' Why could you not have told me yourself, that morning you walked to the station with me ? ' he asks suddenly.

' Told you what ? '

' That you were going to marry Mansfield.'

' But I wasn't—I had not thought of it—

he had not even asked me,' I rejoin in a breathless jumble.

A puzzled look comes over Allan's face.

'But you were thinking of it then?' he insists. 'You meant to marry him if—if things did not turn out well with me.'

'I don't understand you in the very least,' I return slowly, staring at him with wide-opened eyes. 'I never dreamt of marrying any one else until you—until you—— Oh! er—well, I am sorry you did not like India.'

For Bryan here makes his appearance at the entrance from the ball-room, and saunters jauntily up to us.

'Of course he did not like India! Nobody ever does ; only if a fellow *has* to stay there, he generally makes the best of it. Is there room for me on that bench, darling? Well, Sir Allan, have you been arranging with my wife when you are to come to us?'

I am fully aware that I deserve no sympathy. What wife does who begins a sentence to a man which she cannot finish in her husband's hearing? Who, loaded with that husband's benefits and kindnesses, owing everything in the world to him (even the very gown upon her back), yet feels furious anger when he unconsciously interrupts the pleasing assurance she is giving her quondam lover, that she has only married the unfortunate man as a last resource.

Allan mutters something indistinctly in reply to Bryan's question. What do they mean about his coming to us?

'Any time after your return from the North would suit us, provided it is this side of Christmas, on account of the shooting. The first week in December, eh?'

'What is it you two are plotting?' I break in hurriedly.

'Mr. Mansfield has been kind enough to ask me to stay with you,' says Allan, looking defiantly at me. 'Have you any objection?'

I gaze at him in astonished silence—too

full of joy to speak. So I need not say good-
bye to him to-night; without any planning of
my own, Fate is arranging some delicious days
for me.

I shall have him in my own house; there
will be endless opportunities of talking to him,
not a beggarly quarter of an hour snatched
from a ball-room, and already interrupted by
Bryan—by Bryan!

Ah! My eyes fall guiltily, and a shudder
runs through me.

'Have you any objection, Mrs. Mansfield?'
repeats Sir Allan.

I answer not; but my husband chuckles
amusedly, and, with a fatuous laugh, exclaims—

'Any objection! She is delighted, I know
—and Frances too.'

Frances too! It is not Fate, then, but
Frances, who has made this arrangement.

Her unaccustomed smile at Bryan in the
ball-room recurs to my mind.

It is quite possible she and Sir Allan have discussed it all beforehand, and in my over-weening self-consciousness I have nearly been a marplot.

'Of course I am delighted,' I echo, lifting my eyes again and smiling carelessly ; 'and when you come to stay with me, Sir Allan, I won't entrap you into cold-catching draughts. The North Pole would be quite stuffy after this corridor. Shall we go back to the ball-room ?' with an amiable all-round turn of the head which amply includes Bryan.

# CHAPTER XXIX

## INVITATIONS

THE wheels of the carriage which brings Frances home are crunching the gravel outside ; inside I am lounging over the drawing-room fire and paying the penalty of last night's excitement in every member of my aching body. I listen apathetically to the banging of the front door and the bustle of the servants ; as the returning wanderer has made so very free with the house, and chosen to invite whom she will, I do not feel it incumbent upon me to rush out and fall upon her neck in ardent welcome. So I hug the fire even closer, and pick up a fresh volume of my novel with ostentatious indifference.

'Here you are !' cries Frances. 'Dear

old thing! I am so glad to come back to you!'

And slipping down beside my low chair she envelopes me in a furry embrace. Frances affectionate is an appalling sign; to touch the extreme corner of a cheek-bone is her normal idea of a sisterly caress.

'Your boa is in the fireplace,' I rejoin stolidly.

'You are looking very tired,' she continues, throwing her outdoor garments pell-mell around the room and crouching down upon the hearthrug close to my skirts. 'The ball last night was frightfully dull, wasn't it?'

'It was. I will pour out some tea for you.'

Whereupon I march away and trifle over the tea-tray, Frances following me, and trickling forth a stream of ingenious flattery. My house is so artistic and comfortable after Mrs. Stuart's ramshackle, Irishlike, untidy abode; I was so lovely last night, that she

was quite proud of being my sister; all the
men were admiring me, and all the women
were pulling me to pieces; my diamonds
made Lady Dromore's family tiara look like
a steel fender; my gown bore Worth's signa-
ture all over it, &c. &c.

When she pauses at last, even her cool
effrontery a little dashed by the impassive
reception of her various remarks, ' Well,
Frances,' I say listlessly, ' you are very polite
this afternoon. What is it you want?'

Two big tears appear as if by magic in my
sister's clear eyes; she has the gift of tears,
and can weep copiously over nothing at all at
a minute's notice.

'How hard you are to me, Esmé!' she
murmurs reproachfully. 'I am in such
trouble, and so lonely; I have no one to help
and advise me, if you won't.'

I know she is fooling me, just as well as I
know that she is sitting there. But her small
face really does look very drawn and white

this afternoon ; she is all I have in the world —well, after Bryan, of course; and if I am miserable myself, is that any reason why I should make her miserable too?

Is not this a heaven-sent occasion for acting up to all those lofty resolutions which I make so freely in my good hours, and which have such a hideous trick of utterly vanishing from my mind at the moment of need?

'I don't want to be hard to you, dear,' and I stretch out a friendly hand; 'only I wish you would be more open with me.'

'Then I will be open with you,' cries Frances quickly, throwing her arms around me and pressing her cheek against mine. 'I will tell you everything. It is Allan Vaudrey who is making me so miserable. Oh, Esmé, I am so fond of him!'

I try to disengage myself, but Frances holds me tight and hurries on—

'Really fond of him for himself, not for

his money—and I do think he likes me too;
but I am afraid you will be so against it all.'

This affectionate position must be promptly
abandoned.   Frances can feel every beat of
my heart against hers, and as it sounds in my
own ears like a runaway steam-engine, she
must have a pretty accurate guess at the
breathless emotion which is choking me.   So
I push her firmly away and sink down into a
chair behind me.

'Of course I do not forget that you liked
him yourself ages ago; but so much has happened since then, and you have settled down
so comfortably with Bryan, and—and yet,
Esmé,' with clasped hands and tragic pose, 'if
you tell me that you still love Sir Allan I will
give up all thought of marrying him for your
sake, however much I mày suffer.'

'What nonsense you are talking!' I rejoin
sharply.

'I shall be only too delighted if you will
assure me that it is nonsense.   You have com-

plained that I am not open with you. Now I
have told you all there is to tell, and it is for
you to decide.'

'To decide what?' I ask. 'It seems to
me that this is a question for Sir Allan—not
for me.'

Frances' face dimples all over—it never
struck me before how conceitedly she can
smile.

'Of course it is a question for Sir Allan.
But I, for my part, could have nothing to say
to him that would cause you unhappiness.'

'Make your mind quite easy on that score.
You and Sir Allan can say what you like to
one another. It won't affect me in the least.'

'Really and truly?' cries Frances, ex-
ecuting a delighted pirouette. 'Well, that's
settled then. And he is coming here the week
after next?'

'The week after next.'

'Bryan will shoot all the best coverts, I

suppose.  Don't you think we had better have a house-party?'

'No doubt about that,' I rejoin dryly.  'It would be a little difficult for the poor man to hit it off with the three of us *en famille.*'

'Whom shall we ask?  The Lucans?  The Sandford Somersets?  The Fitzgeralds?'

But at each name I shake my head.

'I will not have any of that lot.  Very likely they might be kind enough to come and take Bryan's shooting; but they have been too rude to us since we left Billington.'

'I dare say,' returns Frances, opening her eyes; 'but who has not been rude to us? You might as well retire to a desert island at once if you are going to cherish such an inconveniently long memory.'

'I wrote some notes this morning.  There is a list on my writing-table.'

'Sir John Seymour, Colonel Beckett,' reads out Frances; 'they will come fast enough— they are never overburdened with invitations, whatever they may say. Miss Jolliffe, Archie Sinclair, Mr. and Mrs. Carslake. The Yarboroughs! Esmé, you are not in earnest. You haven't really written to them?'

'I have indeed; and the note is posted. I always told you I meant to ask them here.'

'But why, why, why?' cries my sister in an excited crescendo. 'What has induced you to saddle yourself with such an outrageous couple?'

'Because they saddled themselves, as you elegantly express it, with us for months together, at a time when no one else cared to remember our existence.'

Frances eyes me disgustedly.

'There is a strong element of priggishness in you, Esmé. However, if the note is really posted it is no use my saying any more.'

Bryan is wildly interested in his first shooting party.

He has hung around my writing-table the whole morning, and I have been glad that

Frances was out of the way (having views of my own as to the guests to be desired); for, much as Bryan dislikes her, and slightly as he ranks her charms and graces, he yet has a profound admiration for her social tact and a high opinion of her diplomatic powers.

'When shall we get the answers to those invitations?' he speculates presently, his mouth full of plum-cake and his heart full of joy ; he has returned from his afternoon ride in time for tea, and picks up the conversation exactly where he left it off at lunch. 'The day after to-morrow, eh ?'

'By return of post from most of them, you may be sure,' answers Frances with a sneer.

'Why do you say that?' asks Bryan, turning uneasily towards the oracle. 'I should imagine, from what Esmé tells me, that they are all people with many engagements and little spare time.'

'I am sorry to disagree with Esmé,' says

my sister politely, ' but if Colonel Beckett has a previous engagement when he is invited anywhere, it will be the first time I have heard of such an unusual event ; and as for Sir John Seymour——'

' Didn't you tell me this morning that Colonel Beckett commanded the 100th Hussars and was a great friend of the Prince of Wales?' demands Bryan of me with a puzzled air.

' He certainly commanded the 100th Hussars once upon a time,' I rejoin firmly, and then tail off weakly into, ' and as for the Prince—well, of course I haven't heard his version of the friendship, but there is no doubt that Colonel Beckett got his regiment through him in some way.'

Bryan leans back much relieved, but Frances has not finished.

' He had some appointment in India which would have brought him in contact with the Prince when he went out there ; and the worthy Colonel is such a terrible old bore that they gave him the 100th Hussars and shipped him home to get rid of him.'

She has not made much of a point as yet. The fact of Colonel Beckett's connection with his Royal Highness, slight and unflattering though it be, is established ; and Bryan is satisfied.

'We all know there is a good deal of jealousy about these things,' he remarks toler-antly. 'But perhaps you were right, Esmé, in thinking that the blue room would do for Colonel Beckett. I proposed the white-panelled room this morning,' explanatorily to Frances ; 'there is no doubt it is the best single bedroom—but now I suppose we had better set it aside for Sir John Seymour, eh ? '

'Don't you think we might wait until we know who are really coming before we decide upon their rooms ? ' I suggest evasively.

It is trembling on the tip of Frances'. tongue to remark that Sir John will not recog-nise himself in so fine a chamber; and were she not anxious to keep in with me just now, Bryan would be hotly informed that only the very waifs and strays of our acquaintance are being invited to his house ; and indeed, had it not been for the dire necessity of filling up a background to an awkward quartette, not even they would have been bidden to my table.

'I should have liked a peer,' says Bryan mournfully, helping himself to a large piece of buttered toast. 'To have a lord staying in the house would have been very nice. I wanted Esmé to ask the Earl and Countess of Greyshawk. I know they used to be a great deal at Billington—I have heard the Rolands talk about them ; but she says it would not be etiquette to ask them here, as she has seen nothing of them since her marriage.'

His lament is interrupted by the appearance of Dixon, looming large and stately in the doorway. Dixon, unlike his master, has lived in houses with many lords, and, by delicate hints and dimly veiled regrets, frequently and heaps of people (always changing, so that one has not time to tire of them), and all that is going on in the world communicated *vivâ voce*, so that one may be kept up in everything without ever looking at a newspaper.'

'Good Heavens!' ejaculates Allan, as I pause rather out of breath.

' Ah! you are shocked. You think all good women love the country. For my part, I don't see why a woman should be any the better for having nothing to occupy her mind but pigs and poultry, and her neighbours' doings, and her servants' misdemeanours. I am sorry to lose the least fraction of your good opinion ; but, if it is built upon any mistaken notion that I have innocently rustic tastes, its foundations are in the sand.'

I can hardly believe my own ears that I am thus easily chattering to Allan Vaudrey, and that he is looking down upon me with an appreciative smile—that smile which tells a woman that any nonsense she may utter is pleasant hearing. We seem suddenly and causelessly to have returned to our old positions with one another.

'As to one's good opinion,' says Allan with a laugh, 'I can't see that it is more merited by attention to the pigs and poultry than by devotion to society.'

Then with an abrupt change of voice he asks—

'You are fond of children, are you not?' After a moment's pause I answer him coldly—

'No,' and turning my head away gaze miserably over the dripping fields. For his question and the tone in which it is asked make a familiar ache, always dully present, spring actively to my throat and tighten it to pain.

Am I fond of children? Why not ask me if I am fond of other women's husbands or their lovers? Why should I care for *their* children? But a child of my own! Oh Heaven! how I

# CHAPTER XXX

## WITH THE GUNS

IT is the morning of December 5th—grey, wet and muggy. Four women, clad in typically British garb—sad-coloured Newmarkets, stout high boots, and sparely trimmed hats—eye one another curiously in the outer hall at Milbourne.

'How hideous we all look!' I ejaculate discontentedly.

'Just like four men out of a Noah's Ark,' giggles Miss Jolliffe.

Miss Jolliffe is tiny, gay, and inconsequent. To compare her with a canary would be unjust to the mental ballast of a well-educated bird.

'We should look much worse in half an

hour's time if we started in any other get-up,'
avers Jacquetta.

' At any rate, let no man's gaze behold us,'
I say persuasively. 'Let us go for a consti-
tutional and keep out of the way of the
shooting.'

' We can't do that,' declares Frances.
' They have arranged the whole beat for us
to see Hackett's Wood shot, and we can't
change our minds now.'

' The gentlemen would be so disappointed,'
protests Jacquetta. ' Joseph always says he
shoots twice as well when there are ladies
looking on.'

I submit with more than resignation.
Nowadays I am never in the same mind for
two minutes together. At breakfast I proposed our going out to see the shooting; a
minute ago I wanted to go in the opposite
direction; but had they all agreed with me, I
should have grown heavier and duller with
each step that took us away from the guns,

and spent the whole morning in inwardly cursing my waywardness.

Our guests arrived yesterday; three women —Jacquetta, Mrs. Carslake, Miss Jolliffe—and six men. I think I received them with decent smiles and due civility; I cannot have said anything very inappropriate or *mal à propos*, for they have none of them betrayed any astonishment at my demeanour. Indeed, Jacquetta has complimented me upon my bearing.

'You have changed since your marriage,' she said to me last night. 'Your face has grown gentler and you take more trouble to please.'

I am glad she thinks so—glad that my lunacy has not yet reached the fast-threatening pitch of making me utterly deaf to all voices but one, utterly unseeing of all but one presence.

Allan has arrived in a mood which my old nurse would have described as 'masterful.'

From shunning me, he has suddenly gone to
the opposite extreme of monopolising me with
bold assertion. Whether he has been meditating upon my interrupted confidence at the
Brackham ball, or whether he is simply tired
of treating me like a child in disgrace, I know
not ; but he has openly assumed a possessive
air which thrills me with delight and terrifies
me at the same time. Heaven help me if my
prudence and propriety are to be the only
bulwarks against scandal!

'I can't tell you how glad I am to see you
so happily settled, my dear,' remarks Jacquetta,
as we tramp along the beech avenue together.
'Mr. Mansfield was saying last night that he
should always feel grateful to Sir Joseph and
me for having brought you together ; and I
am sure you ought to thank Providence for
giving you such a model of a husband—so
kind, so devoted !'

' Bryan is very good to me,' I respond with
a sigh.

'Marriage is a great lottery,' pursues Lady Yarborough conversationally, 'and it is not everyone who draw such prizes as you and I. The next thing is to find a second Bryan Mansfield for Frances.'

'She is very young yet. This is our way, over this stile.'

'Those shots seem very close,' says Jacquetta uneasily. 'Which way are they shooting?'

But she forgets her nervousness the next moment in the ecstatic sight of her Joseph, proudly elevated on a little knoll and blazing away recklessly right and left.

'He will bring down some game too big for the bag,' whispers Frances to Miss Jolliffe. 'Look at that beater dodging from tree to tree. They ought to pick out a bachelor brigade for him.'

'Mark!' screams Lady Yarborough excitedly. 'Look! that must be one of

Joseph's birds fluttering down there in the road.'

I positively envy Jacquetta her interest in her husband. Why am not I marking the birds of my legitimate gun and vehemently admonishing a small boy to pick up that running pheasant which he has winged, instead of anxiously squinting around the corner of the covert where a stranger in an iron-grey Norfolk jacket is dealing out slaughter and destruction?

'Sir Allan is making the bag,' murmurs Miss Jolliffe. 'That is the third time he has wiped Sir Joseph's eye.'

'How happy they all look!' says Frances. 'And how degrading to be a woman! I shall shoot, too, as soon as I am married, but I don't think it is good policy in a girl.'

As she speaks her eye glances critically over Major Johnstone, who has handed his gun to a keeper and is coming towards us.

With unerring *flair* Frances has noted Allan's change of manner, and is already preparing to herself a buffer wherewith to break her fall. I heard her tell Major Johnstone at breakfast that she considered woman's mission in life was to keep a constant eye on the cook, and make man comfortable in the house; which appropriate sentiment awoke an immediately responsive thrill in the gallant major's bosom, he being notoriously fond of his creature comforts.

'And I think a book ought to be kept with the *menus* of each evening's dinner carefully and fully written out, even to the sauces, so that there may be no monotony,' she concludes, with intent earnestness.

'By Jove, yes! That's a good idea. But between you and me and this mustard-pot, Miss Nugent, it isn't often one finds a young lady with such sensible notions. Most girls seem to think tea and toast enough to live upon.'

He makes straight for her now, and it
would not surprise me to hear that they discussed the relative merits of bread sauce and
bread crumbs, à propos of the pheasants he
has just slain during the whole walk from
Hackett's Wood to the copses which are to
be shot next.

'You are walking in the wet, Mrs. Mansfield,' says Sir Allan's voice behind me.
'Come over here; this is quite a decent
path.'

A decent path! It is a bumpy, slippery
little track, from each side of which the long
grass moistly swishes my petticoats—nevertheless, to my perverted taste, an Elysian
promenade.

'How nice the rain on the grass smells!'
says Allan, bucolically sniffing.

'I hate it! A nasty, green, damp, rural
smell. The scent I like is the *odeur du pavé*
—a nice, towny, sociable smell—that suggests
cosy theatre parties, and unlimited shopping,

and heaps of people (always changing, so that one has not time to tire of them), and all that is going on in the world communicated *vivâ voce*, so that one may be kept up in every-thing without ever looking at a newspaper.'

'Good Heavens!' ejaculates Allan, as I pause rather out of breath.

'Ah! you are shocked. You think all good women love the country. For my part, I don't see why a woman should be any the better for having nothing to occupy her mind but pigs and poultry, and her neigh-bours' doings, and her servants' misde-meanours. I am sorry to lose the least fraction of your good opinion; but, if it is built upon any mistaken notion that I have innocently rustic tastes, its foundations are in the sand.'

I can hardly believe my own ears that I am thus easily chattering to Allan Vaudrey, and that he is looking down upon me with an appreciative smile—that smile which tells a woman that any nonsense she may utter is pleasant hearing. We seem suddenly and causelessly to have returned to our old positions with one another.

'As to one's good opinion,' says Allan with a laugh, 'I can't see that it is more merited by attention to the pigs and poultry than by devotion to society.'

Then with an abrupt change of voice he asks—

'You are fond of children, are you not?' After a moment's pause I answer him coldly—

'No,' and turning my head away gaze miserably over the dripping fields. For his question and the tone in which it is asked make a familiar ache, always dully present, spring actively to my throat and tighten it to pain.

Am I fond of children? Why not ask me if I am fond of other women's husbands or their lovers? Why should I care for *their* children? But a child of my own! Oh Heaven! how I

would love it ! How I should worship the little
arms that would always stretch out to me ; the
little voice that would call me mother : the
dear little body which would be to me so immeasurably more precious than anything in
the world !

But the expectation, which many wise
people have, that women of decent feelings
should be devoted to children in the aggregate,
always appears to me incompatible with my
human nature, at any rate. Allan stalks silently
along—disappointed, perhaps, that I am again
below the accepted feminine standard.

' But I have immense sympathy with
anxious mothers,' I go on lightly, as soon as
that horrid lump in my throat will let me. ' I
think a woman absorbed in her nursery is
certainly to be pardoned. The creature who
sins beyond forgiveness is the woman who talks
about her servants. Don't you agree with
me? '

' Indeed I do,' says Allan energetically.

'She deserves an end like that of the weak-minded female who committed suicide the other day, being driven thereto by the worry of them.'

' Not really ?' I ask laughing.

' Really,' nods Allan. 'I saw the finding to that effect of twelve good men and true in print—so there can be no room for doubt.'

'After all,' I meditate dolefully, 'we should never laugh at anything a wretched *woman* lapses into. Poor creatures, women are, without occupation, without scope for ambition, without an individuality of their own even, identified as men's wives or daughters, judged and classified according to their nearest masculine belongings, and placed here or there as the case may be, and told to amuse themselves. As if this world were a place for amusing oneself! The only solid lasting happiness seems to me to come from work—and how are women to find work, educated and encouraged as they are to dawdle their lives away?'

Allan looks a little dumbfounded as I launch my diatribe at his head. He, poor fellow, has never had occasion to investigate feminine woes, and, like most motherless, sisterless bachelors, nourishes a vague idea that women's requirements are always to be met by a little affection and a great deal of money.

' How contradictory you are this morning ! ' he exclaims. ' First you enlarge upon the delights of running about town, and now here you are demanding a mission ! '

'I am not demanding a mission,' I say, laughing a little at his puzzled face, ' and I am not contradictory—wordy if you like ; and yet not half so wordy as I could be upon the subject. But I would rather hear something of your plans than harangue you like this. What are you going to do ? *You* ought to have a mission with all your money.'

'Well, I want to do some good with it,'
he returns slowly; 'but I am a little vague as
yet. I must go carefully into the whole
question—how the money is made, the condition of the workpeople in the North, and
the state of the factories. Then I shall
know exactly what surplus I have to work
with.'

'And then?' I ask, half pausing in my
walk, for we are nearing the copses. I am
anxious to hear all about his work and his
future. Will it become so absorbing, so interesting to him that he will forget me? I
would not wish him to carry about with him
in perpetual unrest that sick longing which
torments me; but it will be hard to pass
utterly out of his life.

Even while I look at Allan a change comes
over his face. Cool consideration vanishes,
and he bends his eyes on me with a passion
there is no mistaking.

'*Now* comes before *then*,' he answers

harshly. 'Before I leave this place I am going to have it out with you.'

As we stand gazing at one another in the dripping rain, Frances and Major Johnstone pass a little to our right.

'He was reading them extracts from the "Police Manual,"' guffaws Major Johnstone, evidently trotting out his one ewe lamb of a story for Frances' delectation.

'It is the funniest thing I ever heard in my life,' she responds, with a ringing laugh. But her face belies her words; the laugh is forced, and she casts a look of white apprehension towards Allan and me. The sight of her recalls the jealous tortures I have suffered.

'What are you going to have out with me?' I ask, with an uneasy smile. 'Do you want my consent to your flirtation with Frances?'

To which Allan vouchsafes no reply.

'You know you *have* been flirting outrageously with her,' I persist uncomfortably.

Still no answer.

'And indeed I have been trying to get accustomed to the idea of you as a brother,' I continue, in a lachrymosely miserable voice.

'Good Lord! How can you stand there and say such a thing to me?' exclaims Allan suddenly. 'You know very well I have only been using her as a blind—I did not want to get you talked about!'

'Well, here we are at the copses,' I remark indifferently as the rest of the party joins us, and pulling my umbrella over my face to hide the happy smiles which are breaking forth. 'Will it put you out if I stand here while you are shooting?'

'Not a bit,' he replies.

Nor does it ; he shoots as straight as man can, and I, watching behind his arm, am more than ever convinced of the superiority of his sex. If I held the gun, and Allan were standing by me, though I were at other times the most brilliant, the surest of shots, yet on this occasion would the pheasants fly unharmed and the hares run scathless.

'I wouldn't talk so much to Sir Allan if I were you,' says Frances, when we are wending our damp way homewards, having left the men to the cheerless carouse of a stand-up lunch in the rain. 'You know people are so quick to make remarks. Miss Jolliffe asked just now if he was your own particular or merely a casual.'

'Vulgar little creature!' I interrupt angrily; and then refrain from further abuse of my guest, as it strikes me that Frances is probably only following the ingenious example of Mrs. Gamp in fathering upon her friend any little remark it does not suit her to own to.

# CHAPTER XXXI

## TOO FOND A HUSBAND

WHAT is it that Allan is 'going to have out
with me'?  What ashes does he want to rake
up?  There is no earthly good to be gained
by harping upon the weakness which sepa-
rated us, by tantalising ourselves with rehearsing the existence which might have been.
There is nothing to 'have out with me.'  He
went away and left me; I married another
man.

Not a heroic record on either side; what
use to con it over?  Allan would only say
bitter things to me, and I—no meek Griselda
at any time—should tell him that the man
who deserts a woman, as he deserted me, has
lost all right to reproach her.

No, it is a thousand times wiser to leave the past alone. Let us take all the sweetness we can out of life, and upon the ruins of our love build up a friendship firm, close, and enduring.

Allan must come and stay with us a great deal in the winter; in town we shall meet every day; when we go abroad he can always run over and join us.

I can get along very well for a while if I am sure of meeting him again at some given time—it is the uncertainty that kills.

Of course there will be talk about it; people do chatter so, and put horrible interpretations upon the most innocent trifles; but with Bryan always with me, no harm can really be believed.

It is not an ideal existence to picture to oneself; but it is the best that remains.

And not wrong. There would be nothing wrong about it. I should be a better wife to Bryan if my mind were more at ease and my nerves less on the stretch. I could say my prayers night and morning more peacefully if the one great desire of my heart were not always thrusting itself in unsatisfied longing between Heaven and me. Allan must never murmur one word which the whole world may not hear, never touch me with the slightest caress.

What wrong can there be in such a friendship ?

So I argue with myself while a Babel of small talk goes on around me.

Frances is unusually quiet this evening ; but Miss Jolliffe is as conversational as a magpie, and Jacquetta rivals her in volubility, being much excited at the visible proof our establishment affords of her social tact and discretion.

'Lovely old silver, isn't it ?' she observes to Sir Allan at dinner. 'I declare I am as pleased to look at it as if it were my own. When I think of that dear girl there,' nodding

her large black head towards me, 'and the
plight she was in this time last year, it does
my heart good to see how perfectly happy she
is now.  She positively has everything one
could desire.  Mr. Mansfield tells me this old
glass is priceless; they picked it up by chance
in Venice when they were honeymooning.'
Then, in sudden fear of having wronged her
host, she adds confidentially—'Not that there
really was much "picking up" about it, I
expect; Bryan Mansfield is not the man to
haggle over a few francs—and if there were
any question of getting what dear Esmé
fancied, he would not let money stand in the
way.'

'Very devoted of him,' returns Allan with
a sneer.

'Devoted!  Ah, you may well say so!  It
is my belief he worships the very ground she
walks upon,' exclaims Lady Yarborough with
a tender sigh.

Why are fat people always so terribly sentimental?

'And happily all the devotion is not upon one side,' she continues. 'He told me last night that a fonder, more affectionate wife, man could not wish for.'

Allan, frowning without disguise, is angrily pushing the salt-cellar about in a way which augurs ill to the 'priceless old glass' in front of it. How foolish of him to mind Jacquetta's chatter! He must learn not to pay any attention to such nonsense.

'Oh no, no, you won't easily shock me,' cries Miss Jolliffe airily across the table. Sir John Seymour has been telling some slightly *risqué* anecdote, and has apparently been afterwards seized with remorse. 'I have just been staying in the fastest house in Perthshire— and you know that means a good deal. All the women came without their husbands, and the men without their wives; and they tossed me in a blanket on the lawn because I was the only unattached person there.'

'What does she mean?' whispered Jacquetta to Allan. Jacquetta's honest, middle-class mind has been considerably puzzled two or three times to-day by Miss Jolliffe.

'Does she mean that she isn't engaged to any one?'

Lady Yarborough confides to me afterwards in the drawing-room, that she could not get any satisfactory answer from Sir Allan. 'But he agreed with me that Miss Jolliffe seems a little fast. I hope she won't have any bad effect upon Frances. Young girls are so easily influenced, and any talk about flirtations between married people is so very demoralising. Don't you think so, dear?'

Jacquetta has not forgotten sundry passages between Frances and Sir Joseph at Riverdale which did not meet with her approbation; but she will have no cause for jealousy now.

With cool determination Frances has already made clear to Sir Joseph the fact that she has no time to spare for dalliance with him. She has no further need of his house and his protection; therefore why waste her breath upon useless talk with so uninteresting a mortal? .

It has not taken long to disenchant him. He was never in love with Frances, though very much in love with the reflection of his noble person which he was wont to behold in her flattering eyes. Since he arrived yesterday she has persistently turned a deaf ear to his lordly conversation, and has on two separate occasions deserted her chair when he has placed himself near her. Less than this would have damned her in Sir Joseph Yarborough's estimation.

'Poor little Francie's head is quite turned by your success, my dear Esmé,' he remarks, eyeing her contemptuously from afar; 'but if she wishes to attain to your position she must first discard her present flightiness of manner.'

No one else would accuse Frances of flightiness at the present moment. She is seated in a high-backed chair, and is gazing up at Major Johnstone with Madonna-like gentleness of expression.

She has been hard at work upon her fluffy fringe, which is much less pronounced than usual, and a black gown finishes the metamorphosis from the frisky damsel of yesterday into the staid English maiden of to-night.

She came into my room before dinner to borrow the aforesaid garment; her own wardrobe does not include a black frock, and we can always wear each other's clothes.

' He told me this afternoon that he thought women never looked so well as in black,' she informed me; 'he evidently likes them to bear the impress of domestic virtues written all over them. Well, I have damped my hair, and I am going to part it in the middle—and,

by the way, Julie, you go and tell Dixon that
I will come down presently and mix the salad
myself for dinner.'

Already her voice had assumed a mild
whine, and the corners of her mouth were
decidedly pulled down—usually they curl up
on her cheek in a most impertinent fashion.

Her efforts are crowned with success.
Major Johnstone is minutely describing to her
each hole and corner of the place which came
to him with his grandmother's money, and is
asking her opinion as to whether a small room
over the ice-house should be used as a dairy or
larder.

She is voting in favour of the larder,
when Allan makes his way across the room
to me.

' Come and show me the books in the
white library,' he whispers persuasively.

But I shake my head. Though bearing
the most inviting aspect, with two roaring fires
casting changeful lights upon the many-

coloured volumes which line its walls, the white library is tenantless.   I dare not march into it alone with Allan.

' Do,' he begs.   ' Please do.   I particularly want to talk to you.'

' And I want to talk to you ; but I won't go in there now.   You may come for a walk with me to-morrow morning if you like.'

' All right,' with eager assent.   ' At what time ? '

' I will be ready at half-past eleven in the hall.'

Allan tugs reflectively at his moustache. ' I am afraid of your sister cutting in if we start from the hall,' he remarks ungallantly. ' She is watching us now.'

So she is, with stolen side-glances, and is straining her ears to catch what we say, if I mistake not.

' I will be in the peach-house at a quarter to twelve,' I murmur, under cover of a burst of laughter from the other end of the room, where Archie Sinclair, with the aid of two candles and a large sheet of kitchen paper, is drawing Miss Jolliffe's profile on the wall.

'Come, Esmé, and be done too,' calls out Bryan. 'It really is a wonderfully good likeness.'

As I join him obediently he strokes my cheek with his forefinger, and says—

'Not that black and white could ever do justice to this,' in maudlin tenderness.

Now I have insisted upon a distinct understanding with Bryan that there are to be no affectionate demonstrations in public. In private I submit to his endearments with what patience I may ; covenanting only that he is not to touch the tip of my finger before other people. I have obtained this from him by emphatic assurances that the slightest caress is extremely bad form ; but the delightful excitement of his house-party has, unhappily, driven my injunctions from his mind.

'Eh, Sir Allan ? A black-lead pencil and

a piece of white paper won't give any idea of all this pretty flesh and blood, will they ? ' patting my chin and neck with fond proprietorship.

I jerk myself wrathfully away, nearly knocking over Miss Jolliffe, who is staring open-mouthed at Bryan's blandishments.

' How touching ! ' she exclaims, with her light, twittering laugh. ' How edifying ! And how long have you been married ? '

' Nine months,' says Bryan solemnly ; ' and let me tell you, Miss Jolliffe, I have never regretted my marriage for one single instant. It was the wisest thing I ever did in my life.'

And pulling down his white waistcoat with emphatic assertion, he looks proudly upon his shrinking chattel and the assembled company. Bang—bang goes the door behind us ! Sir Allan Vaudrey has left the room.

# CHAPTER XXXII

## THE ASSIGNATION

ALLAN is waiting for me at the door of the
peach-house—waiting in anxious impatience,
for it is five minutes past twelve and I am
twenty minutes late. Frances has been sticking to me like a leech ever since breakfast, and
Bryan has been worrying for instructions as to
the disposal of his guests.

'Leave them alone,' I have adjured him with
repeated insistence. 'If you want people to
enjoy themselves, leave them alone.'

'But there's Miss Jolliffe sitting all by herself in the hall,' he rejoined on his last irrup-
tion into my boudoir. 'Don't you think I had
better ask her to go for a walk with me?'

'She won't thank you if you do; she is

hanging about until Archie Sinclair comes out of the smoking-room, on the chance of his asking her to play billiards.'

'Oho! that's it, is it?' exclaimed my husband, looking very knowing. 'Well, then, shall I see if Colonel Beckett would like to go over the Home Farm?'

'Yes, do.'

Some victim must evidently be offered on the shrine of his fussiness, and why not Colonel Beckett? After all, I think he will probably enjoy his morning walk. Bryan is an excellent listener, and will not discover any inaccuracy in the extraordinary statements with which the gallant soldier invariably garnishes his conversation—not even if he informs him, as he did me at breakfast, that he dined out thirteen times last week.

Frances has been more difficult to shake off; but at length I have evaded her and am hurrying along the holly walk which leads to the peach-house, fastening my fur coat as I go.

'Thank Heaven!' exclaims Allan with
unnecessary fervour as I complete my hasty
garbing under his eyes and thrust my cold
fingers gloveless into my muff. ' I was beginning to give you up, and if you had not come
I should have marched indoors and asked the
reason why.'

'You must not be so impatient,' I
chide, smiling up into his face, and wondering within myself at the comfortable sensation of being so happily at home which
suddenly takes possession of me. What a
terrible power it is which makes every
action, every word, every gesture even of
Allan's, fraught with interest to me and full
of matter for thought! Nothing less than
an aberration of one's faculties can cause the
very wave of the hand of another human
being to be so absorbing a subject for reflection!

' I have been patient too long,' says Allan,
answering my smile with a frown. ' It would

have been better for us both if I had been more impatient a year ago.'

' Oh, a year ago!' I exclaim with a deprecating shrug of the shoulders. ' What is the use of talking about a year ago? It will only make us very cross.'

We have left the kitchen garden and are pacing along the laurel walks which lead out to the park.

' Never mind,' says Allan, unheeding my remonstrance. ' I want you to tell me yourself, with your own lips—and not through another person this time—how you could have had the heart to throw me over so suddenly. For it was sudden ; you cared for me that morning we walked to Riverdale station together—I'll swear you did ! '

' *I* throw you over ! How can you say so? It was you who threw me over. Of course I cared for you ! '

' Then you did not send me that message ? '

' What message ? '

'Telling me not to come and see you any more.'

' I never sent you such a message. Who said so ? Who said so ? '

' Sir Joseph Yarborough, of course.'

'Sir Joseph Yarborough ! ' And panting with excitement, my breath coming short, I turn and face Allan. ' I never sent you any message through Sir Joseph Yarborough. How could you think I would do such a thing ? '

' You never sent me any message through Sir Joseph Yarborough ? ' repeats Allan, turning very pale. ' You never asked him to tell me to keep away ? '

' Oh, Allan, there has been some horrible mistake ! ' and breaking down I suddenly burst into tears.

But Allan shakes me roughly by the arm.

' Don't cry,' he says harshly ; ' but listen to me. The very morning after my father was buried Sir Joseph came to see me, asked how I was placed, and, when he found that I had only 10,000*l.*, begged me in your name not to give you the needless pain of refusing to marry me.'

'In my name!'

'Yes, in your name. Do you mean to tell me you knew nothing of his request?'

'This is the first I have heard of it. How could you be such a fool as to believe him?'

'He was so circumstantial,' groans Allan. 'I questioned him over and over again, and only became more convinced that you must have told him everything. He alluded to my walk with you that morning, and said that he hoped I would not press any advantage or admission I might have obtained from you at a moment when your feelings towards me were excited by compassion.'

'Why, he must have been eavesdropping! I never told him anything.'

'Did you tell anyone about it?'

'Only Frances. Ah—h! I see it all now!'

And, with lightning-like quickness, words, gestures, looks that have puzzled me for many a long day become clear to my mind.

'Frances is at the bottom of it all!'

I remember her constrained manner that day when Sir Joseph Yarborough went up to London; her fright when she heard of Allan's return from India and arrival at Mrs. Stuart's; her attempts to keep us apart—attempts which seemed successful at first and which have been growing fainter as she becomes convinced of their uselessness.

'Frances!' repeats Allan incredulously. 'What motive had she for interfering?'

'She did not want me to marry a poor man. She wanted me to marry Bryan.'

'That was another thing Sir Joseph told me,' continues Allan bitterly; 'that you had said you would rather marry Mansfield than be dragged into a long engagement with me.'

' Oh, Allan, how *could* you believe such things of me? I would not have believed anything other people said about you. I would have insisted upon seeing you my-self.'

' It is very easy to say that, and of course I see now that I was a fool; but at the time I had no doubt whatever that Yarborough was speaking the truth.'

' He thought he was,' I cry eagerly, ' and that made him all the more effective a messenger. I can trace Frances' finger throughout. She primed Sir Joseph and he went off to you, genuinely believing every-thing he said. He has not wit enough to be a good' hypocrite.'

Allan here consigns my sweet sister to per-dition, with an oath not loud but deep. As for me, I have not time to waste over her; I am not surprised at anything she has done—I know her so well—and 1 will deal with her afterwards. Just now I am all absorbed in the plot which has robbed me of happiness, and I question Allan lengthily and minutely.

'You had always told me how much you thought of money and everything it represented,' he says presently. 'You had never pretended to be indifferent to the good things of the world. I had always seen you surrounded with every possible luxury and had always known that you wanted to make a good match. All this came back to me when Yarborough said you had declared that you could never stand love in a cottage.'

'Oh, Allan, if I have been worldly I am bitterly punished for it! How much happier I should have been with you in the poorest hut!'

'It is very easy to say that now,' he repeats bitterly.

'Indeed I never doubted it!' I exclaim eagerly. 'Don't be hard upon me. Really and truly I had not one thought of marrying Bryan until I heard you had gone to India—

and I felt so forsaken ! You know I had no-
where to go, and I was very uncomfortable in
Sir Joseph's house.'

'Poor little darling !' says Allan relenting.

Then we walk along in sad silence. The
'might have been' is dangling so tantalisingly
before our eyes.

'At least I am very thankful to know the
truth,' I say at last. 'You can't imagine how
it has hurt me to be compelled to think badly
of you. I almost feel as if you had been given
back to me.'

'I know the feeling,' he rejoins quickly.
'I left England cursing you, your worldliness
and your weakness ; never doubting a word
Yarborough had said. But the more I thought
about it the more puzzled I grew. The look
in your eyes and the smile of your mouth
kept haunting me until I felt that if you were
indeed as false as I had been told I could
never believe in human faith and love again.'

'Poor fellow !' I murmur softly.

'So I came here to see how you were taking things, before I settled to my work in the North.'

'Thank Heaven that you did!' I exclaim. 'And now you must never leave me for long again.'

Allan shoots a quick glance at me, but says nothing.

'I don't want to interfere with your work or to keep you always dangling at my apron-strings,' I continue, with quite a cheerful laugh—the plan of intimate friendship I have sketched out recurring consolingly to my mind; 'but you must come and see me very often, and when you are away you must write to me and tell me what you are doing. So that, whenever we are obliged to say good-bye for a little while, we shall know that it will not be long before we meet again.'

No response from Allan. Surely he does not think me forward?

'You can't be working for ever, you

M 2

know,' I urge ; 'you will be obliged to take some holidays, and they must always be spent with us.   You must send your horses here in the winter—Bryan will be delighted to put them up.   Then you must run up to town a little in the season—you will get so rusty if you don't—and we shall be there, of course.'

Still no answer.   Allan does not like my plan.   He must like it.   He must!

'I will take such interest in your work, Allan,' I plead, my voice beginning to quiver in my anxiety.   'You will tell me everything you are doing, and perhaps I may be able to help you in some parts of it ; there are often little things that a woman sees quicker than a man—and I would think of nothing else.'

I raise my hand to his coat sleeve, but he turns his head away.

'You are imagining perhaps that Bryan would not like it ; but indeed you are mis-taken.   He would not mind in the least—why

should he? He is not at all jealous or sus-
picious—and indeed what would there be for
him to suspect? He will always be pleased
to see you—Why don't you answer me? You
*must* do what I want. Oh, Allan, don't be
unkind to me—I am sick and tired of suffering, and I cannot live without you!'

'Nor I without you!' exclaims Allan;
and turning round he seizes me in his arms.
'But what a child you are to propose such a
plan to me! No, no, my darling! my way is
ever so much better. You must come with
me and be my very own.'

With all my strength I endeavour to free
myself from his grasp, but he holds me firm,
and I only succeed in so far drawing back
that I lean against his hands, which are
clasped behind my waist, and look up into his
eyes.

'Don't, Allan, I beg and implore you—
don't say anything like that to me again. It
will only separate us for ever!'

'Nonsense!' he says roughly. 'We have been tricked and deceived. We must do the best we can for ourselves now. Trust yourself to me, my own love, and you shall never regret it; you shall be as happy as the day is long.'

And he tries to draw me closer to him, but, placing my hands against his shoulders, I resist firmly.

'I should never be happy if I did such a wicked thing as that.'

'Then you don't love me as I love you,' with an impatient shake.

'We are different, I suppose,' I sigh; 'I should be perfectly miserable if I did what I knew to be wrong. But, dear, there is no harm in what I propose—and we should be a great deal together. *Please* do what I ask you,' with a piteous attempt at coaxing.

'It is quite impossible,' says Allan firmly; 'I wonder you don't understand that. How could I stand by and smile when you are that fellow's wife? Any man would tell you the same.'

'Then I think you are very selfish,' I cry, falling to abuse in my trouble and despair. 'You know how utterly miserable I am, and you refuse to give me the least help or comfort.'

'I refuse to give a promise which I have not the power to carry out. The position you propose is impossible. I ask you to come with me, and if you will not I must go alone.'

'Allan, you *know* we should not be happy.'

'*I* should,' he returns doggedly. 'I should be happy with you anyhow and anywhere!'

I am mute in utter hopelessness—not wavering one hair's-breadth in resolution, but tortured with grief. Allan takes my silence as a sign that I am yielding, and suddenly bending down kisses me passionately on the mouth. As his lips touch mine a thrill so responsive tingles through me that I tear myself

from him in sudden alarm; if he kisses me
again I shall lose all power of resistance, I
shall do whatever he bids-me.

'Let me go this instant! I mean it. Let
me go!' I cry violently.

Slowly and grudgingly he opens his arms
and releases me.

'I do not ask you to stay now,' I pant,
moving backwards and placing the width of
the path between us. 'You had better go—
and at once!'

Happily for me, Allan mistakes my agitation and imagines, with true masculine pene-
tration, that I am simply angry at being
kissed!

'I beg your pardon,' he says, in a tone
which he endeavours to make formal, but
which is merely furious. 'I will not offend
again, and I will leave your house at once.
Mr. Mansfield ought to be complimented on
the extremely correct behaviour of his wife.'

And raising his hat he turns on his heel and leaves me.

'Oh, Allan, don't go in anger!' rises to my lips; but I check the exclamation in time. I am too weak to provoke a second encounter.

# CHAPTER XXXIII

## HE IS GONE

'My dearest Esmé, how very ill you look!' exclaims Bryan at luncheon, pausing in his researches into the anatomy of a woodcock. As he is of course at the other end of the table and has to raise his voice to attract my attention, he naturally attracts the attention also of our intermediate guests, and my poor white face is immediately focussed by nine pairs of eyes. 'You have knocked yourself up walking yesterday. She always wants to do too much,' he adds explanatorily; 'her mind is too active for her body.'

'How is it that we are none of us angry at being told that our mind is too much for our body?' inquires Frances, throwing herself compassionately into the breach. ' We should be furious if it were said that our body was too much for our mind.'

' " Mens sana in corpore sano " ; that's the thing we ought to pray for,' quotes Colonel Beckett instructively. ' Clive wrote it with his own hand under his portrait in the Council Chamber in Calcutta.'

' Did he now ? ' ejaculates Miss Jolliffe. ' Well, it wasn't modest of him then. He should have left that for someone else to do.'

' It is a motto which I have made my own,' continues Colonel Beckett, unconsciously imitative in one point at least. 'Summer and winter I rise at five to pursue my studies ; three mornings of the week are devoted to German Grammar——'

' Three, four, five,' counts Bryan loudly, from the head of the table. ' I thought so ! We are one man short. Who is it ? Oh ! Vaudrey. Where is he, I wonder ? '

Dixon steps forward with dignified self-possession.

'Sir Allan desired me to inform you, sir, in case you inquired for him, that he has walked into Fairley to see if an important telegram which he is expecting has arrived. He also wished me to say that he never takes any luncheon.'

'But the telegrams are always immediately brought by hand,' exclaims Bryan. 'You know that, Dixon. Why didn't you tell Sir Allan?'

'I did acquaint Sir Allan of the fact, sir, but he seemed impatient and anxious to inquire for himself. I asked him if he would have the dog-cart, but he said he would rather walk.'

'And he doesn't take any luncheon! Dear, dear!' ejaculates Bryan, with a compassionate sigh.

'There's nothing extraordinary in that, my dear fellow,' remarks Colonel Beckett. 'I never take luncheon myself—only if one is in the house with ladies it is more cheerful to accompany them to the dining-room.'

He is eating steadily of each possible dish, and it would not be hard to predict that he will be still lingering over the sweets when everyone else has finished.

I am sitting in dazed silence. The thought of absenting myself from the table has not even occurred to me, and I eat, drink and answer when I am spoken to, like a woman in a dream. The feel of Allan's arms and the touch of his lips are infinitely more real still than the forms and voices around me.

'You had better go upstairs,' whispers Frances sharply, as we leave the dining-room. ' I can say you took a chill yesterday.'

But I will not do that. I will not lose the last sight of Allan, the last tones of his voice. What do I care what these people think?

' No, I would rather sit over the hall fire all the afternoon, and see if I can't get rid of

my cold that way,' I answer aloud, mindful of
the fact that the hall fire commands a full
view of comers and goers, and quickly appro-
priating my sister's suggestion of a chill for
the benefit of the company in general.

'You look as if it had gone to your bones,'
says Jacquetta, scrutinising me closely. 'I
have got my little medicine chest upstairs—
you know I never go anywhere without it; do
let me give you some aconite globules.'

'That would be very kind of you,' I assent
meekly. I would swallow a whole bottleful
of aconite globules without any inquiry as
to the results, if they would only leave me
alone.

'It was foolish of you to go out in the
damp again this morning,' chimes in Miss
Jolliffe. 'It *was* you I saw going towards the
kitchen garden about twelve o'clock, was it
not?'

'Very likely,' I reply, as indifferently as I
can, and stooping over the fire to conceal the

hot blush which is mounting causelessly to my face. 'But I wish you would not all be so kind and sympathetic, it only makes me feel worse. I assure you I find that the best thing for a cold is to take no notice of it.'

'Then you can't have very bad ones,' pants Jacquetta, who is breathless from a hurried rush upstairs to the medicine chest. She is horribly frightened lest I shall change my mind before she can get the globules down my throat. Why is the love of physicking their fellow-beings so firmly implanted in the breasts of so many good women? When all the others disperse for their afternoon walk or drive, Jacquetta positively insists, in spite of my energetic remonstrance, in bringing her knitting and sitting down beside me—so tenderly does she feel disposed towards her rare patient.

'I am going to drive along the road to Fairley and pick up Sir Allan,' Bryan informs me on his way to the stables. 'He couldn't have known it was fourteen miles there and back when he started.'

Bryan with his guests is like a hen with ducklings ; he would fain keep them quacking all around him.

'Let me fetch your embroidery,' says the good-natured Jacquetta. 'I know you don't like to sit still and do nothing.'

'No, don't trouble, thanks,' I reply hastily, 'it would worry me just now—I mean I don't feel well enough to work—a cold makes one very lazy, don't you think so?'

And I wander miserably to the west window which overlooks the Fairley lodge. My head aches, but my body feels hideously light—as if it did not belong to me. Allan may change his mind during his long solitary walk. He may possibly come back and say that he will accept my terms and keep to my conditions. Shall I have strength of mind to send him away if he does?

'I wouldn't stand there in the draught of

the window, if I were you,' cries Lady Yarborough warningly. 'You know the first
thing for a cold is to keep in one atmosphere,
particularly after taking aconite. Come back
to the fire and I will tell you all about the new
curate at Riverdale ; we think he will marry
Eva Fenton.'

As the afternoon light begins to fade the
dog-cart drives up to the door and Bryan
enters the hall, dark, and rounder than ever in
his ulster, Allan frowning, tall and fair, over
his shoulder.

'We will just put the matter to my wife,'
Bryan is saying. 'She is a person of sound
common sense, aren't you, Esmé, darling?
Here's Sir Allan, who declares he must be off
at once ; he has had a telegram from his agent
in the North, requesting his immediate presence
there on important business. Now what I say
is this ; as the agent has done so long without
him he can surely do a day or two longer.
Isn't that likely, eh ? '

I have risen in my nervousness and stand facing them both. I open my lips to reply, but only a vague, husky murmur comes forth, which sounds like ' So sorry ! '

Happily for me, Jacquetta is one of those worthy people who are always ready to chorus. She choruses now.

' How tiresome ! What a provoking agent ! But I wouldn't give in to him, Sir Allan, if I were you. I would send a reply telegram asking him what he wanted me for. Wouldn't you, Esmé ? '

' Yes—no—perhaps he wouldn't like to telegraph,' I stammer.

' Now you really must give up the idea of going this afternoon,' insists Bryan, ' and we can all talk it over this evening. Eh, Esmé, mustn't he ? ' Then finding that I am not the vociferous ally he had hoped for in his pressing hospitality, ' I don't know what Frances would say, I am sure,' he adds feebly. ' Where is Frances ? ' looking helplessly around, as if

she were hidden behind the window curtains.

'I assure you I must go at once,' interposes
Allan firmly. 'Thanks all the same. If I look
sharp, and you will be so kind as to send me
to the station, I shall just catch the five
o'clock express. My man can follow with my
things whenever it is most convenient to you.'

'The dog-cart is there and you can take it
of course; but I do think you are spoiling
your agent. Come now, wait till to-morrow at
least——' and Bryan is still murmuring his
remonstrances when Sir Allan puts out his
hand, touches mine as if it had been a hot
potato, says good-bye to Lady Yarborough
and turns his back on us both.

'Most unfortunate thing!' says Bryan as
he returns to the fireplace, after duly speeding
his parting guest. 'He was out-and-away our
best gun and we are going to shoot the Home
Covert to-morrow. If he had stayed I should
very likely have been able to send the bag to

"The Field"—and there's no hope of that now. Why didn't you back me up, Esmé? turning round in most unwonted fault-finding; as a rule all I do or say is perfect in my husband's eyes. 'I thought your manner to him decidedly rude—almost as if you wanted to get rid of him. He's a nice enough fellow, I am sure; he will never set the Thames on fire, but you mustn't expect too much from a baronet with a large fortune. You might have been a little more cordial.'

'Poor Esmé is not well,' interposes Jacquetta. She is all the more ready to defend me from the fact that she is not over-pleased with my husband's remarks upon his guns. The idea of anyone shooting better than her Joseph!

'Isn't she? Aren't you, dear?' inquires Bryan, all tender solicitude in an instant. 'By Jove, you do look dickey! Poor little thing! You ought to go and lie down at once.'

'I think I will,' I answer, catching grate-
fully at his suggestion. 'No, don't you come
with me; my head is aching so—I am better
alone.'

When I reach my own room happily
and fortunately no temptation to tears assails
me. I pace up and down with dry, wide-
opened eyes and that curious sensation of
lightness in my limbs, as if the laws of gravi-
tation were temporarily suspended and I could
as well walk the air as the solid earth. I
rehearse my interview with Allan, from the
moment I met him at the peach-house until
he turned and left me. Not one inflection of
his voice, not one turn of his head has escaped
me. 1 recall the look with which he said
'Trust yourself to me, my own love,' and the
tone in which he declared, 'I should be happy
with you anyhow and anywhere.' Memory is
all that is left me now to live upon. I may
never see Allan again. As the years roll on
he will be consoled, and some other woman

—fairer, maybe, and sweeter than I—will be his wife and the mother of his children ; while for me dull duty is all that remains, made duller and harder by the sharp contrast of the happy lot that might have been mine.

But at any rate I cannot be robbed of memory. Allan has told me he loved me, his arms have pressed me, his lips have kissed me. Every day I shall remember that.

It is odd that I don't feel inclined to cry. I usually cry so easily—a quick word, the sight of any trouble or illness will always move me to tears ; but this afternoon I have said good-bye to happiness, and here I am perfectly dry-eyed.

When the first gong sounds I proceed to dress carefully and puzzle my maid by the unusual amount of jewellery I put on. Bryan likes to see me be-diamonded. I must try more than ever to do what pleases him. Poor Bryan ! It is hard that a man should lavish all his love and tenderness upon a woman and get nothing in return. Yet he is no worse off than we all are, I suppose. We all of us have our troubles. It is a cruel world.

'What a heavenly *rivière* !' chirrups Miss Jolliffe as I meet her on the stairs. 'You are a happy woman to possess such diamonds. But my goodness! what is the matter with you ? Your eyes look as if they saw a ghost.'

'It is only the effect of my cold,' I reply with a smile. I am sure that smile was right. I was so painstaking over it.

'Well, after all, some people's colds come out in a worse fashion,' reflects Miss Jolliffe impartially. 'I always get stone deaf.'

## CHAPTER XXXIV

### SIR JOSEPH'S INVITATION

It was Wednesday when Allan went away. Thursday, Friday and Saturday have to be got through with these people in the house. I do not betray myself; of that I am certain. They may think me dull—Miss Jolliffe indeed hints, not distantly, that the building of my gowns and the decoration of my house has absorbed my wits—but it never dawns upon my guests that they are to me as shadows while someone hundreds of miles away is the reality. I smile persistently through each dinner at Sir John Seymour's well-salted stories, thereby earning from him the doubtful encomium that he is glad to see I haven't any starched nonsense about me; I smile less persistently but with well-timed accuracy during each luncheon as Colonel Beckett overwhelms me with ample details of his sporting tours in India and his pedestrian feats in Norway. At breakfast it is not necessary to smile so much ; no one expects vivacity at that mistakenly public meal, and a vacant amiability answers every purpose.

During each day, hunting, driving, walking, I make one long continuous effort ; and when they depart on Saturday afternoon not one of the party, I venture to say, has the least suspicion that their hostess was invited to run away from their host last Wednesday, and has been torn in pieces ever since by a mad regret that she could not reconcile it with her conscience to do so.

The Yarboroughs are to remain over Sunday. Sir Joseph complained yesterday so pointedly that he h d had no chance of a quiet talk with my husband, that I was obliged to ask them to stay on. I know he and Bryan

used to have long business conferences at
Riverdale; but Bryan has rather shunned him
here, I am afraid. I should not like to seem
ungrateful to Jacquetta and her husband, and
I bear him no ill-will for the unwitting share
he took in deceiving Allan. He was only the
catspaw of a cleverer person.

Frances has carefully kept away from me
since last Wednesday. Needless to say she
has not been deceived by Sir Allan's telegram
from the North, nor blinded by my studied
gaiety. She knows well enough that the truth
has come out at last, but beyond her unusual
avoidance of me I have no sign of her consciousness. For this I am thankful; I want
time to consider how I am to treat her in
future, and for the present all my energies are
absorbed in putting an outwardly fair front
on my trouble by day and in bemoaning my
misery by night.

My conversational efforts become even
more toilsome on Saturday evening. Flatness

falls upon our little party ; and if it were not
for the fondly lingering interest with which
Bryan dwells upon his departed guests and
discusses them with Lady Yarborough, I
should be reduced to quotations from the
poets in order to dispel the gloom of silence—
Sir Joseph and Frances not being upon speaking terms.

'That Miss Jolliffe wouldn't be a bad-
looking creature if she weren't so thin,'
remarks Jacquetta, as we sit over the fire after
dinner.  'But she is terribly flighty.'

'You don't know, perhaps, that Miss
Jolliffe is a first cousin of the Duke of Bir-
mingham ? ' returns Bryan tersely reproving.

'Is she really ? ' inquires Lady Yarborough, much impressed.  'Why then she
must be an Honourable !  I wish I had
known.'

'I don't think she is an Honourable,' confesses my husband reluctantly.  'I looked it
all out in the Peerage before she came.  She

is the daughter of Lord Adolphus Jolliffe, who was the younger brother of the late duke.'

'She must be the Honourable Miss Jolliffe if she is the daughter of a lord,' argues Lady Yarborough with growing excitement.

They are safe now for ten minutes, as it will take Bryan all that time to rehearse the proofs from Debrett which sadly convinced him that the lady in question had no claim even to the slimmest of titles.

How lonely it will be for Allan in that big empty house of his at Bramblecope! He has gone straight there, I am sure. I wonder if the north wind is howling as madly at his windows to-night as it is here. His work will absorb and interest him in the daytime, I expect, but he will be horribly alone in the evenings; and I am selfish enough to hug the consolation to my heart that he will sit and think of me in those quiet hours—perhaps even close his eyes sometimes and imagine that I am sitting by him.

'So you see she is highly connected on both sides,' finishes Bryan.

'Well, I will say for her that she gave herself no airs,' declares Jacquetta. 'She always waited for me to go out of the room first.'

Sir Joseph Yarborough is gazing silently into the fire. He has not been his usual impressive self during this visit; perhaps his crow is apt to get uncertain out of the charmed precincts of his own farmyard. At any rate, it is in a comparatively subdued voice that he now remarks—

'We shall all go to church to-morrow morning, I suppose; but I hope, Mansfield, that you have no engagements in the afternoon which will prevent your giving me ten minutes' quiet attention to business.'

'I shall be delighted, my dear fellow,' returns Bryan nonchalantly. 'Sir John Sey-

mour is an amusing chap, isn't he, Lady
Yarborough?'

'Very,' says Jacquetta. 'But I couldn't
see the point of some of his stories. What
was the joke about the bishop who did not
eat any dinner one evening because he
thought he had paralysis? Sir John said
that he was really pinching the leg of the
lady who sat next to him all the time instead
of his own. But I don't think that is very
funny. It must have given the poor bishop
a terrible fright to think he had lost all sensation in his leg.'

'The point is that the lady never objected,'
explains Bryan gravely. 'She was rather
flattered, don't you see?'

'Oh!' says Lady Yarborough, much
shocked. 'I didn't understand that part of it.'

I cannot help laughing at Jacquetta's
scandalised face. The indelicate edge of Sir
John's story has to me been rubbed off by
long familiarity; it was a favourite joke of

Uncle Frank's in the days of my childhood.
So I begin to laugh, genuinely amused at
first—how could we stand up against our
troubles if all sense of the ridiculous were
taken from us? But my laugh quickly de-
generates into a *fou rire* painful and prolonged, during which I am more conscious of
Allan's unkindness in pushing matters to so
dire an extremity that we are obliged to part,
than of the original cause of my ghastly
merriment.

'You are getting quite hysterical,' says Lady
Yarborough severely.

'Dear Jacquetta, do forgive me,' I apolo-
gise, pulling myself up with a sharp effort and
wiping the tears from my eyes. 'But you
should have heard Uncle Frank tell that story;
you would have been ever so much more
shocked.'

Next morning as I am putting on my
bonnet for church, Bryan comes into my bedroom.

'Look here, Esmé,' he begins, fidgeting uneasily with my long gloves which lie on the dressing-table. 'Yarborough has got some abominable notion in his head of making me talk business all this afternoon. Now there is nothing I hate so much ; so mind you stick to me like a leech. It is easier to turn the conversation when there are ladies in the room.'

'But he may have something important to say to you—something confidential,' I object, not overjoyed at the prospect of thus spending the long hours between lunch and dinner.

'Well, then, Sunday is not the right day to make a communication,' retorts my husband, trying how far his little finger will go up the thumb of my glove.

'Nonsense, Bryan!' I exclaim, turning round to stare at him in astonishment, it being the first hint I have had of any Sabbatarian prejudices on his part. 'You had much better go into the library with him after luncheon for half an hour and get it over.'

'It is such a shocking example for the servants,' declares Bryan, wagging his head sanctimoniously.

'Why, you might be reading sermons, for all they know! You are spoiling those gloves.'

'You be a good girl and do as I tell you,' returns my husband, 'and I will write to Paris for a boxful of new gloves for you. Miss Jolliffe says they are making them now of a different shade of tan.'

'I don't want Miss Jolliffe's taste brought to bear upon my things,' I retort ungratefully; 'she always looks as if her own clothes were bought at a fair and put on with a pitchfork. Well, if you are so anxious for my society all the afternoon, you shall have it; but I think you are treating Sir Joseph rather badly. Have you any idea of what he wants to say to you?'

'None whatever,' avers my husband.

' But you know how bad for me all business is. That was the one thing my doctors agreed upon—I have told you so before—that I was not to be bothered about business.'

I submit to his wishes accordingly—my conscience pricks me less when I am making myself uncomfortable to please him ; but very uncomfortable and undignified I find it to be the persistent third when one of two people anxiously desires my absence. I sit by Bryan's side in the hall after lunch.   I accompany him in the stroll Sir Joseph  proposes later on ; we pass the peach-house and laurel walks in our ramble, and at that moment I should have stoutly refused to leave Bryan, even had Sir Joseph demanded it of me point-blank.   But my ardour cools as the afternoon wears on, and when poor Sir Joseph rises after tea and says, in imperative tones, ' Now, Mansfield, if you will come into the library with me for a quarter of an hour, I shall be much obliged,' I fix my eyes on the carpet in front of me and studiously avoid the look Bryan throws over his shoulder.

'If you really wish it,' he responds with a reluctant cough; then rises slowly and pauses. 'You come too, Esmé,' slipping his hand through my arm. 'You can answer those notes you got this morning.'

'There is no need to disturb Esmé,' exclaims Sir Joseph hastily. 'It is a mistake to trouble ladies with business.'

'I have no secrets from my wife,' declares Bryan, with much dignity; 'and I like to have her with me.'

'I must request you to give me an interview *alone*,' persists Sir Joseph. 'I cannot go thoroughly into our money transactions in a lady's presence.'

Thus cornered, my husband turns feebly towards me. Jacquetta and Frances are looking on in silent curiosity. For Bryan's own sake I must not shelter him any longer behind my petticoats.

' I forgot to tell you that I answered those notes before church,' I remark, with elaborate unconsciousness; and as I draw my arm away from his compelling hand I give him a little push forward. 'So that I am quite free now to play to Jacquetta.'

The interview is a long one, the quarter of an hour which Sir Joseph had demanded stretching itself out into more than fourfold, until the first gong disturbs their conference.

' May I come in ? ' I ask, tapping at Bryan's door as I hear him enter his dressing-room. 'You are not vexed with me, dear, are you? I did not go into the library with you only because I thought it looked so very bad—so marked.'

' It does not matter ; it would not have made any difference,' answers Bryan absently. His face is flushed and his expression, usually so impassive, strikes me as scared.

' What is it all about? ' I ask curiously. ' You might tell me, Bryan. I will not talk of it.'

'The old fellow gave me some money to invest for him twelve months ago, and now he is bothering me about giving up the securities —obstinate old fool!—when he is getting high interest.'

'What interest?'

'Eight per cent.'

'Dear me! that is very high, isn't it, Bryan? What did you invest the money in?'

'Now, my dear child, what possible difference can that make to you? For Heaven's sake, don't you begin to bait me too. I am bothered enough already about money without having to give explanations at home.'

'I don't want you to give explanations at home,' I answer gently. 'I know I don't understand business affairs; but if you are at all short of money we ought to economise, I think. We are spending it like water just now. I should be quite willing to shut up the house and go abroad for the winter if you wished it.'

'You are a good little soul,' says Bryan,

looking queerly at me. 'Yes, it is very likely we may have to go abroad. But whatever you do, don't say a word to anyone.'

I am not at all inclined to say a word to anyone about Bryan's money transactions; they interest me too little. If he suddenly informed me that we were reduced to extreme poverty I verily believe I should receive the news with resigned indifference. I imagine that the human capacity for trouble is limited, and if one's mind is full to the brim of passionate regret and longing, minor details, such as the loss of a carriage, a French maid, a fine house, but feebly swell the overflow.

I am, however, sufficiently alive to my surroundings to be very glad when the Yarboroughs take their departure on Monday morning by the first possible train after breakfast. Sir Joseph has been behaving like a bear with a sore head since his interview with Bryan. He has utterly refused to be drawn into any conversation with either Frances or my husband; he has snapped at Jacquetta, and has been civil to me only. I am uneasy rather than gratified at this mark of distinction, seeing that I resigned myself long ago to the cold shadow of his disfavour. Can he be suffering from tardy twinges of remorse at his officious interference in my love affairs? Yet that would scarcely have prompted him to come back from the door after saying good-bye, and after Jacquetta had been warmly tucked up in the corner of the brougham, and remark to me—

'I hope you will remember, my dear Esmé, that my house is always open to you, and that should—er—circumstances—er—ever render it desirable for you to return to my roof, I shall be delighted to receive you.'

I am too astonished to find a suitable reply before he again takes his leave, for good this time. What 'circumstances' could possibly render it desirable for me to return to his roof?

# CHAPTER XXXV

### 'NOTHING TO DO'

Now that the Yarboroughs have gone I am thankful to be able to drop my mask and subside into utter listlessness.

With Frances and Bryan there is no need for feigning. Bryan would never guess anything that was not told him in so many words, or presented to his outward vision in black and white; and Frances knows too much to be imposed upon by spurious cheerfulness.

So I fold my hands in front of me and give the reins to my regrets.

The consequence is that at the end of three weeks my body is always tired, my appetite has disappeared, and my bones begin to start out in unaccustomed places.

One morning Julie announces to me that she has been obliged to reduce the bodices of madame by a whole inch, and is disgusted to find her news received with laughter. I cannot help being tickled at the idea that, like Glorvina, 'all me frocks have to be taken in.'

By slow degrees a curious, hard resentment against Allan comes over me. It is so cruel of him to go away and abandon me to my trouble simply because he cannot bear the sight of my husband always by me. He prefers to leave me rather than endure worry. He chooses to remain in ignorance of what is happening to me day by day. I may be well or ill, glad or sorry, he does not know; and as time goes on he will not care.

I had a nasty kick on my ankle, at a crowded meet last week; but for the stirrup-iron it must have been serious, and, as it was, my habit was cut through and my foot bruised. Bryan was in genuine distress. At the end of two days when I would fain have forgotten the whole subject, he was still running it to death with objurgations upon the careless groom who rode the offending horse, with devout wishes that his own ankle rather than mine had received the injury, and with recommendations of drastic remedies compared with which the original bruise would have been a trifle. For all Allan knows, I may be killed out hunting any day ; he has rejected all communication with me.

And so—it being but sober truth that ' to be wroth with one we love doth work like madness on the brain'—I fret and torture myself by alternately dwelling with grim insistence upon his selfishness, as I angrily call it, which has dug a bottomless abyss between us ; and then weakly falling into hour-long reveries in which I picture him beside me with such vividness that I can almost feel the touch of his lips on mine.

Sometimes a strong desire to write to him assails me ; not a love-letter, but just a few

friendly words centred around a plausible
excuse. It would be easy to find one. He
left a tiny pencil-case in the drawing-room—
what more natural than that I should send it
to him? Ordinary civility would necessitate
a reply ; and how I should welcome even the
curtest note!

I do not yield to the temptation. I *cannot*
control my thoughts, struggle as I may ; but
I can and will control my actions. The
pencil-case, lying where he left it, has become
the most precious object in the house to me ; it
is on a little table beside my own particular
chair, where Allan put it one day when he had
been making a rough sketch of an Indian idol.
Fifty times I have wondered what I should do
with that pencil-case ; and at last I find myself
actually concocting a note which might with
the utmost propriety accompany it to its
owner.

This will not do. I put on my wraps, and
taking the offending object all too tenderly in

my bare hand, walk half a mile to the big pond and hurl it beyond reach in its muddy waters.

How I envy those happy people whose lives are full of work !

In these days of misery and wretchedness which have come upon me it is the utter want of occupation which is the hardest thing to struggle against. If I had only some honest genuine work which must be got through or other people would suffer thereby, some matter of-fact employment which demanded my best attention, I am sure I could control my thoughts in time and bridle my wandering fancy. I dare say there would be moments in which the painful longing for the sight, the touch of Allan, would seize me and assert its mastery ; but hard work would be a powerful rival, and would drive it into the background for at least a few hours of each day.

But how am I to find work ? What am I able to do ? Her house is popularly supposed

to be a woman's kingdom ; but how astonished
the servants would be if I suddenly expressed
my intention of occupying myself with domestic
affairs, and how very uncomfortable everything would become in consequence ! I have
never been able to sympathise with those
worthy ladies who devote long hours to
meditating upon the shortcomings of their
domestics, and I have always noticed that if
servants can do their work at all, they will do
it all the better for being given a free hand.

I make some feeble attempts at visiting
the poor ; but I find that the result in each
cottage is the same. My presence is more or
less politely endured, and the appeal to my
purse is more or less undisguised according to
the character of the occupant.

I order various charitable periodicals from
town, which under diverse headings pretend
to show how sickness and poverty can be
relieved by individual effort at home. It is
the same tale with them all. Their organisa-

tions are all complete and perfect, their band of workers willing and efficient—and they only want money.

At last, to my delight, in the corner of one of the least pretentious of them I find a request for some red flannel jackets for the children of a convalescent home to wear in bed. Eagerly I order the ponies and drive into Fairley, where I spend my last half-crown in buying the necessary material; and the days I pass cutting out and making the little garments (aided and abetted by the astonished Julie) are the most peaceful which have dawned upon me since Allan went away. Still, making two dozen red flannel jackets is not serious occupation for a lifetime.

I meditate long and often upon the course of conduct to be pursued towards Frances. Just at first the desire to be revenged upon her, to make her smart, somehow or other, for that cruel blow in the dark, is overpowering. And vengeance would be so easy. She

has no one to defend her. Bryan hates her,
and would be delighted to hear that I wanted
to get rid of her ; he has often hinted to me
in confidential moments that he finds her
presence a troublesome restraint, and has
suggested that she might spend part of the
year at least with the Yarboroughs.

The sight of her pretty delicately-tinted
face has suddenly grown almost intolerable to
me. How dense I have been not to suspect
her long ago! Is not duplicity written in
every line of her curving red mouth, and
deceit harboured in her slanting blue eyes?
Have I ever heard her express a kind thought
or seen her do one unselfish action ? Surely
retaliation is but just.

But by degrees, saner, better feelings take
possession of me. Who am I that I should
mete out punishment to my sister ? Am I so
open, so candid, that I should arrogate to
myself vengeance upon deceit ? Am I not
sinning in thought each day, each hour,

against God and against my husband—not wilfully, just Lord, but helplessly—oh, so helplessly?

> How can he mercie ever hope to have,
> Who mercie unto others will not show?

How can I pray night and morning, 'forgive us our trespasses,' if I will not add 'as we forgive them that trespass against us'?

So gradually and slowly I forsake all plans of revenge, influenced thereto by vague, childish notions of barter with Heaven; if I forgive Frances, perhaps God will help me and send me, in some mysterious fashion, rest and peace.

I am almost entirely alone just now.

Frances keeps out of my way, feeling, one would hope, ill at ease in my society, now that I know all, and being, besides, fully occupied in getting about to distant meets. She has taken to hunting with the same pack of hounds as Major Johnstone; his country is so much better than ours, she explains, the

going so much freer. Bryan, too, is scarcely
ever at home. He has been up to town
nearly every day for the last month—indeed,
ever since Sir Joseph Yarborough left us.

' Business, my dear, business,' he explains
briefly, when I question him one evening as
to his sudden spasm of activity. 'You could
never imagine the trouble old Yarborough is
entailing upon me by his meddlesome fussiness. I am more worried than I can tell you,
and I look upon his want of confidence as insulting—positively insulting.'

' Why don't you give up his securities and
let him manage his money himself?' I ask,
not unnaturally.

Bryan eyes me with his round vacant
gaze.

'I wish I could,' he returns absently.
' By Jove! I wish I could !'

' Why can't you ? '

' Because—well—because—— Now, look
here, my dear girl, if I talked to you for an

hour on end I could never make you understand the nature of these floating securities—
floating,' repeats Bryan, well pleased with the
word, and making a sort of swimming motion
with his hands—' floating.  But here's something you can understand.  I am going to
have your portrait painted.  There now ! '

'Nonsense, Bryan !  How can you have
my portrait painted down here ? '

'I never said it was to be done down
here, did I ?  No, it is all arranged.  Blakely
is going to do it, and you are to come up
to town with me for sittings three times a
week.'

'What an extraordinary arrangement ! ' I
exclaim.  'If you want me to be painted,
why can't you leave it till we go to town in
the spring ? '

'There's no knowing what may happen
between now and the spring,' returns my husband with Delphic vagueness.

'And you told me the other day that you

were short of money! Bryan, do put it off, please. Blakely is the most expensive man you can go to.'

'I am perfectly well aware of that,' says Bryan importantly. 'I am not going to have any second-rate fellow painting my wife.'

'But the money——' I begin again, when my husband interrupts me impatiently.

'I don't know what has come over you lately, Esmé. You used to be the easiest person in the world to get on with ; but now you are always arguing. I tell you the money for your portrait is as a mere drop in the ocean one way or the other, and I have set my mind on it. It is hard, I must say, that just when I am worried to death out of doors, you should suddenly take to crossing me at home.'

Whereupon I collapse into abject submission. I am wronging my husband, all uncon-

sciously to him, in such deep though subtle
fashion, that I am over sensitive to any reproach he may choose to make. And, after
all, how can I judge business matters of
which I know nothing ? Bryan has thrown
out some extraordinary hints lately, but he
must have plenty of capital to fall back upon.
Uncle Frank used always to groan, and say
he was utterly ruined as regularly as each
harvest was gathered in, and nothing ever
came of it. So I accompany my husband,
meekly enough, to Mr. Blakely's studio the
very next day.

'I want him to paint you in one of your
new Paris gowns,' explains Bryan on our way
thither, ' but he won't commit himself to anything until he has seen you. Mind you
describe to him that yellow brocade La
Ferrière sent over the other day.'

But Mr. Blakely pronounces for black,
in spite of Bryan's glowing account of the
treasures of my wardrobe.

'Black!' exclaims my husband disgustedly. 'Why, every woman has a black gown, and you have no idea how much smarter she looks in colours.'

'I will do you in transparent black against a grey background,' muses Mr. Blakely, gazing at me with his head on one side and smoothing his long hair contentedly down his cheeks. 'I have long wished for a fit subject for black.'

'At any rate she must have her diamonds on,' interposes Bryan eagerly. 'I forgot about the diamonds; they will show up well on black.'

'I need scarcely say that you will be entirely without ornaments,' remarks Mr. Blakely, as absently as if he were deaf.

'Conceited ass!' ejaculates Bryan as we leave the studio, after some further discussion as to the accessories and size of the canvas. 'If I had known he was going to give himself these idiotic airs I would have stipulated for the choice of the gown before I took you there.'

'After all, dear, black is very safe,' I say soothingly; 'and you know he might have insisted on something much worse. He would do old Lady Morgan as a Swiss peasant, and her husband did not like it at all.'

Upon hearing which awful fate Bryan consoles himself for my sable garb; at least he has escaped the indignity of seeing his wife depicted as a peasant.

So, three days a week, I drag my weary body up to town; I am nearly always tired now, though I used to be such a strong girl. At first I hate going; but one day as I drive past the hospital for children, which stands about half-way between the station and Mr. Blakely's house, the happy idea occurs to me that perhaps they will let me spend some time there every afternoon on my way home. It would make me almost happy to think I could be of the least use in amusing one sick child.

To my great delight, I am heartily welcomed ; the hospital is in an out-of-the-way neighbour- hood, and not overrun with fine ladies.

Instead of dreading my days in town, I now look forward to them. During the sittings in the morning I may rest and let my thoughts wander without hindrance or inter- ruption—Mr. Blakely, by the way, is making the shadowiest, most emaciated of studies, all eyes and cloudy black draperies—and in the afternoon, for a while at least, I forget my troubles and my regrets in watching bright smiles upon thin little faces and listening to confidential prattle in childish voices.

# CHAPTER XXXVI

## DUNNED

CHRISTMAS has come and gone.

By will of the servants and not from the least desire of our own, we have dined upon coarsely gigantic turkey and deadly plum-pudding, and have had puffy mince-pies placed before us upon every possible occasion. We have endured an extra Sunday thrust unaccustomedly in the middle of the week, and have resigned ourselves to the compliments of the season in varied forms of atrocity. Trumpets have brayed and bells have pealed outside our door in the dead of night ; chorales, lacking the fundamental principle of unanimity, have been yelled in our tortured ears by hoarse voices, and bagpipes have added their shrill tones to the nocturnal clamour.

Our walls have been scratched with promiscuous boughs of holly ; nails have been driven through sacred places by remorseless hands, and from them nooses of evergreen roping hang in reasonless festoons.

Much, and apparently ceaseless, feasting and wassail have been carried on downstairs, for the gait of various individuals whose avocations call them to the back door is invariably more uncertain upon departure than upon arrival.

' I really think we seem to have twice as many posts this week as last ; the postmen must live in the house,' I remark one morning, taking up the second pile of letters that have arrived to-day with a reluctant gesture.

For alas ! alas ! their tale is one and all the same. Outside they differ widely in appearance, from Madame Duchesne's aristocratically sprawling handwriting upon extra cream-laid, gold-stamped, violet-scented note-paper, down to Job Spriggins' niggling little characters upon a dirty blue halfpenny wrapper; but inside their purport is alike. Bills, bills, bills! They all want money; some more, some less; some are content with a brief 'To account rendered,' whilst others hint with thinly-veiled determination that money they must and will have.

Apparently we have paid for nothing since our marriage, for here amongst more recent claims are the backstanding items of goods ordered in London last March on our way abroad.

'For Heaven's sake, don't worry me about those trifles,' cries Bryan irritably, as I venture into the library with half a dozen of the most pressing accounts in my hand. 'I don't know what the tradespeople all mean by dunning for their money within twelve months. Put the cursed things into the waste-paper basket; there are about fifty there that I have shoved in this morning to keep them company. Madame Duchesne, seventy-five pounds; Dreysehoek, a hundred and five, &c. &c. Bagatelles, mere bagatelles! Shove them in and don't worry me for nothing.' Then as I move submissively towards the door, he calls me back.

'Give me a kiss before you go, darling. I didn't mean to speak sharply to you; only I didn't know which way to turn. You will always stick to me, Esmé, won't you?'

'Of course I will,' I answer steadily. 'But I wish you would not keep me in the dark like this. You ought to tell me what is troubling you; something about money, of course?'

Bryan knits his brows and looks out of the window. He is standing in front of a large tin box full of bundles of papers—not letters, but rolls of semi-transparent, whitey-brown paper, closely covered with greenish marks.

'This is what I will do,' he says at last. 'I will tell you everything to-morrow. I am going up to town by the early train, but

when I come home in the evening you shall
know all about it.'

'Come here, Esmé,' calls out Frances, as I
emerge from the library and cross the hall.
'See what a number of robins have collected
around the bread you threw out after breakfast. Come quietly, or you will frighten them
away.'

And as I steal up gently behind her she
stretches out her hand and draws me close,
so that we both look out of the same window
pane. The old familiar touch, grown, alas!
so newly unfamiliar, and the vague, home-
like scent of her hair and gown recall a thousand recollections of our childhood. 'Do
you remember that fat old robin who used to
peck his wife when she came for the crumbs
outside the schoolroom window at Billington?' I ask, rubbing my cheek caressingly
against my sister's. What is the use of coldly
forgiving a person if one is not ready to 'kiss
and make friends?'

'Yes, but after all, when he had finished his own breakfast, he used to keep the others off until she had had hers. A husband is a useful appendage sometimes.'

'How are you getting on with your major?'

'Pretty well. He is hooked, I trust and believe, but not landed yet. He still pulls at the line occasionally, and I sadly want some one to help me with a landing net.'

'Are you going to marry him, Francie?'

'Heaven knows!' she answers with baffling lightness. 'A more eligible than he may appear on the scene before we reach that crisis.'

'I thought you were rather sighing for the useful appendage of a husband just now.'

'So I was,' she confesses frankly; 'but only that he might pay my bills.'

Then, after a pause, during which the reason of her sudden friendliness has chillingly become manifest to me, she says,

'I am awfully hard up, Esmé, dear. Do you think you could help me? Look at these horrid bills I got this morning.' And she pulls a roll from her pocket.

It is a little mortifying to find that she only spoke kindly to me because she wanted money; but the fact is accepted that it is more difficult for the one who wrongs to forget than the wronged one; so I swallow my disappointment as best I may.

'You should have the money this minute if I could give it to you,' I answer, and then pause, hesitating. I must not betray Bryan's secrets to Frances.

'Oh! I know *you* cannot give me the money,' she exclaims impatiently. 'I found out long ago that Bryan does not trust you with cash. But you can ask him for a cheque, can't you? And do you mind not saying that it is for me? He would be sure to make some nasty remarks.'

Then as I stand confusedly before her,

twisting the bills about, she changes her tone
and begins coaxingly—

'Choose your time when you like. I don't
want you to burst into the library this very
moment, and present them at his head like a
loaded revolver. Wait for an opportunity,
and one day, when his cheque book is open
and his heart tender, wheedle a little more out
of him. There, now; I won't take them
back; you try what you can do. And I will
tell you a secret,' with a relieved laugh, as she
sees the obnoxious documents slipped into
a drawer of my writing-table. 'From close
observation of your married life I have laid a
lesson to heart for future guidance, a lesson
which applies in fifty ways, but is comprised
in the one word "settlements." How on
earth we could have been so confiding as to
let you marry Bryan without some arrangement about pin money passes my comprehen-
sion! This fair hand,' shaking her pretty
slim fingers in the air, 'is bestowed on no

man until he has shown a proper sentiment with regard to settlements.'

'If you don't take care you will overreach yourself,' I retort ; 'like the young lady who betrayed such overwhelming interest in the prospects of her children by a possible second marriage that her *fiancé* prudently decamped.'

'Poor thing ! I suppose she had no one to look after her affairs for her,' muses Frances sympathetically.

Next morning Bryan goes up to town by the nine o'clock train and Frances starts a little later for a meet twelve miles off.

'I wish you had been coming with me,' she remarks as she stands waiting for the horses to be brought round ; 'but I must admit you don't look up to such a long day. It is the cold weather, I suppose, that makes you so white.'

'What kind of sandwiches have you got?' I inquire irrelevantly, peeping into her neat little case. It is all very well to forgive and even to forget ; but the author of my changed appearance can scarcely expect her victim to impute it mendaciously to the cold weather for the sake of making conversation with her.

'Pâté de foie gras,' answers Frances. 'I always think *foie gras* is to be earned and not lightly trifled with ; but I shall be six hours in the saddle to-day. Well, good-bye ! Take care of yourself.'

Off she goes, looking as fresh and fair as a daisy or a spring morning—or any other poetical simile applicable to youth and health and unclouded spirits. I have had many qualms about allowing her to hunt alone—she is so gay and pretty ; but, Major Johnstone having declared himself fully persuaded that the constant presence of a dragon is insulting to a young lady's powers of taking care of herself, my remonstrances have been summarily scouted. I am obliged to be content, therefore, with seeing that she has a trustworthy groom and that he is well mounted.

Now I have the long day before me. Since Christmas I have made it a duty to practise for so many hours each morning, to study harmony and to read German; but these self-appointed, self-concerned tasks are unsatisfactory stop-gaps to haunting memory. No one is the worse when my hands slip off the keys and the recollection of Allan's voice fills my mind—my very bodily ears seem often to hear the tones of treasured sentences.

It affects no one but myself if the exercises in counterpoint transform themselves into an imaginary letter in which I beg Allan to come and see me; or if the crabbed German characters carry me back to the old schoolroom at Billington where he and I spent a whole afternoon once looking out the translation of a technical German riddle.

But to-day I will have a holiday. I have not indulged myself in a long, uninterrupted reverie for some time past : I have been living upon snatched half-hours and filched moments.

To-day I will give way to my grief and let my thoughts ramble as they will.

I make my shivering way to the peach-house.

This is how Allan was leaning against the door when I turned the corner of that walk ; he came across that grass plot to meet me. If only once a week, once a month, I could come out here and talk to Allan for half an hour, what a different thing my life would be ! I could endure anything then. It is the utter loss of him which robs me of all strength ; even now, with the short walk from the house, my legs are trembling beneath me. I sit down upon the doorstep of the peach-house and abandon myself to keenest self-pity. What a terrible future lies before me ! Shall I live through it, I wonder, to be an old woman, and will the callousness of age help me to forget the suffering of my youth ?

Nor can I even hope for death. How can I, absorbed in thoughts of my love, pray to be summoned to the nearer presence of the All-pure? Yet, God is merciful; perhaps I am punished now instead of hereafter, for the sin I have committed. For it *is* a sin to marry for money; of that I am certain. And its punishment is speedy. One suffers or one deteriorates.

# CHAPTER XXXVII

## THE REVELATION

THE stable clock is striking three when I hear the crunching of wheels on the drive. From the big window in the hall I make out a station fly approaching the house. It must be Bryan coming home earlier than he expected, for the brougham was to have met him at six.

Poor Bryan ! He has been dreadfully worried about money lately. I hope he will tell me everything presently, and then we can arrange matters upon a more satisfactory basis. We have evidently started our esta· blishment beyond our income ; but it is so simple, so easy to put it all right. Half the servants could work the house quite comfortably; half the horses would be enough for our use—my ponies can be sold and my hunters too; and we will give up all idea of going up to town this season. It is absurd to fret about money when there are such real, such terrible troubles in the world. Only I must have the bills paid; I would make any sacrifice rather than live in debt.

The fly lumbers slowly and heavily up to the front door.

I go forward to meet Bryan; and at the first glance I perceive that something of more importance than mere need for retrenchment is agitating him. His face is flushed, his eyes are wild, and his whole bearing disordered. He has a pile of silver in his shaking hand, and is vainly endeavouring to count out the right change for the cabman.

'Let Dixon pay, won't you, Bryan?' I suggest.

Dixon is gazing open-eyed and jaw-dropped at his master, and as I draw Bryan along the passage towards the library, I am not unconscious of the wink with which that domestic luminary favours his attendant satellites, nor of the upward motion of his hand as of one tilting a glass.

Dixon's suspicions are wide of the mark, however. Bryan has not been drinking. He is simply labouring under intense excitement.

'It's all up, Esmé!' he stammers, grasping my shoulder heavily as I close the door behind us. 'I shall have to make a bolt of it and show 'em a clean pair of heels. It's that confounded Yarborough's doing ; if he hadn't stirred up the whole thing I should have tided it over—for another twelve months at least.'

'You will have to make a bolt of it!' I repeat, parrot-like.

'Yes, I must be off to-night by the six fifteen from Swindon and catch the mail leaving to-morrow morning for Buenos Ayres.'

' For Buenos Ayres—why ? '

' The Argentine Republic, you see. There's no extradition treaty with the Argentine Republic, and I shall be all right there.'

I reach out my hand and touch my own ears and then the sleeve of Bryan's coat. Yes, we are both real. I am not dreaming; and I don't feel astonished in the very least. It seems as if it had all happened to me before.

Bryan is breathing heavily; his eyes never meet mine, but rove wildly around.

' You'll come with me,' he bursts out loudly, as I stand silent before him. 'Say you will come with me—quick! It has all been for you, Esmé. You *must* come with me.'

' Hush ! Don't talk so loud. The servants will hear. Yes, I will come with you.'

Bryan catches me in his arms and presses me passionately to him.

' The worst is over,' he cries wildly, unheeding my caution. 'I can stand anything now. And you shall not want, my darling. There's plenty left to keep you from want.'

I draw gently away. The words do not occur to me to question Bryan; instead, I am reading the present in the light of the past. I have been wrapped up in myself or I should have known something was wrong long ago—should have had my suspicions ever since that morning at Cannes.

Bryan is walking about the room, talking continuously.

'Everything has come together. Yarborough bothering about his hundred thousand; Rhodes' solicitors dunning for the remaining payment for this place; my shares in the Saratanga copper-mine gone to nothing, when I thought they would have pulled me through; my mother's trustees fussing about her investments——'

'Your mother!' I interrupt. 'Have you lost her money too?'

'Every penny of it. But don't you be afraid, darling; there's enough in this' (tapping the tin box which is standing where I saw it yesterday) 'to set us going comfortably out there. And it is a lovely climate, they say; the flowers are wonderful.'

'When did these reverses begin, Bryan?'

'Eh? When did they begin? Oh—ah— well, I really don't know; while I was ill, I suppose. You remember I told you about my illness?'

'Yes; and when you got better you found everything was going wrong?'

'Had gone wrong,' corrects my husband; 'but I thought things would come round again if I left them alone. I made sure everything would shake down all right. You know the doctors told me not to worry——' and he looks at me with a gaze that is half-childish, half-cunning.

'What have we been living on since our marriage?'

'Well, we haven't paid for much. Half of Yarborough's money went in part payment for this place, and my mother's got mixed up in the muddle somehow; only a little of my brother's has been used lately for necessary calls.'

'Your brother's!'

'Yes, but not much of it. There was a tiresome trustee who would not let me sell the stock,' with a regretful accent.

I look at him curiously. How far is he sane? How far is he mad?

'But we are wasting time,' exclaims Bryan impatiently. 'We must be off from here soon —and all this will keep. I can tell you what you want to know later on. We must pack up ourselves; it won't do to let the servants suspect anything.'

Then, as I still sit motionless, he continues apologetically—

'I am very sorry to have to ask you to pack your things, Esmé. I know you have not been accustomed to it. And there is something else I am afraid you won't like. We cannot take Julie; it would not be safe. But you shall have another maid directly we get to Buenos Ayres.'

In the midst of my stunned horror I burst out laughing; it is so funny, so like Bryan, to consider the item of a maid in the midst of dishonour and disgrace.

'I mean it,' he cries eagerly. 'I am quite in earnest. I tell you I have picked up plenty from the wreck to keep you in perfect comfort.'

And again he lays his hand on the tin box.

'In there?'

'Yes.'

'How much?'

'About forty thousand in bonds, and enough cash to take us to Buenos Ayres and keep us for a few days until I can realise.'

'You must leave the bonds behind, Bryan.'

'Leave them behind! You don't understand, my dear girl. I must take them with me in order to get the money out there. Now you had better hurry and pack. I will come upstairs with you.'

'You must only take enough of that money to pay for our passage, Bryan. The rest must go to your creditors.'

'Nonsense!'

'The forty thousand pounds must go to your creditors.'

'And what are we to live upon?'

'We must work.'

'Work!' exclaims my husband with a loud laugh. 'I wonder which would get through most work, you or I!'

Then, patting my shoulder and resorting to a familiar formula, he says—

'Now you leave me to manage the money, and run along and get your clothes together.'

'Bryan, I will not go with you unless you leave that money behind.'

Then indeed my husband turns pale and eyes me with alarm.

'You don't know what you are talking about, Esmé. How could either you or I earn enough to keep us?'

'I could scrub floors and you could break stones on the road.'

'You are ranting,' he says sulkily. 'And as for the money, it would be a mere nothing divided amongst them all.'

'It is no use arguing. I mean what I say. You must choose between the money and me.'

And as I speak a wild inconsistent hope springs up in my heart that he will give me a righteous cause for remaining behind. But Bryan loves me better than money. He argues, he expostulates, he implores, he depicts our certain misery in vivid colours.

'It is so perfectly ridiculous for you to talk of working at all in that hot climate. I hear that people spend the whole day in hammocks, drinking lemon squashes ; I have been making inquiries about the place lately.'

But at last, as the time speeds on and he finds that I will not yield an inch, he begins to show signs of giving way rather than part from me.

' You don't know what you are insisting upon,' he whimpers, ' and you will be terribly sorry for it by-and-by. But I won't go without you ; and if we fool about here any longer we shan't get off at all.'

' Why won't you stay and face it out, Bryan ? It is so cowardly to run away ! '

' Good Lord ! ' exclaims my husband with a start and looking apprehensively over his shoulder towards the door. ' You don't know what you are talking about. No, no !—you said you would come with me if I left those bonds behind.'

' So I will. Give me the box.'

' But the cash for our journey is in it.'

'Then take that out and leave the bonds.'

I stand over him as he fumbles among the papers. His hands are shaking so uncontrollably, and he betrays so strong an impulse to pocket indiscriminately, that I pull the box from him and sort out the bank notes myself. They are all mixed up with the securities, with letters, with odds and ends of paper covered with figures and calculations, even with old invitations ; amongst his treasures Bryan has hoarded a card for Lady Dromore's ball !

'There is the money,' I say at last. ' Will you take care of it, or shall I ? '

' You had better. My head is aching so, I might forget where I had put it.'

I lock the tin box, place it in the big oak cabinet by the fireplace and lock that also. I do up the two keys in a safe packet, addressed to Sir Joseph Yarborough, and enclose one line of explanation ; then I ring the bell and order a groom to ride at once to the post with the precious missive. It will be safe in Her Majesty's keeping.

Bryan meanwhile has gone upstairs, without even taking off the great-coat in which he has travelled. When I enter his dressing-room he is standing by the bed, upon which he has spread out three white waistcoats.

' I can't find any more,' he says helplessly ; ' and I shall want them so in that hot place. I ought to have a dozen.'

I sink suddenly into a chair, and a tight sensation grips my neck. Am I right to take his word for it that flight is necessary? Ought I to leave home and country at his bidding ? Is he capable of judging any business affairs —this creature who, in the midst of ruin and collapse, babbles of white waistcoats ?

A horrid, choking, screaming sound comes tearing out of my throat without volition of my own. It astonishes me as much as it does Bryan, who drops his garments and gapes at me affrightedly.

' Don't ?   For God's sake, don't, Esmé ! '
he implores.   ' It sounds as if you were going
into hysterics.'

Hysterics !   I am ashamed.   I to give way
to anything hysterical!   I thought only un-
educated people with ill-regulated, unbalanced
minds were ever connected with hysterics.

I stamp my heel angrily on the floor, and
regain control of myself.

' I was only going to ask you if you are
quite sure that you must run away like this,
Bryan.   Why can't you go into the whole
thing with your creditors?   You may have
more money left than you imagine.'

' I am quite sure,' he returns sullenly.
' Why will you waste time talking about that
now ? '

' Because I am not convinced that we are
doing what is best,' I say waveringly, more to
myself than to him.

' I *dare* not stay in the country,' bursts
out Bryan desperately.   ' Don't you see that

I should be arrested? A lot of trust-money is missing—and—and—I tell you, Esmé, we must get off by that train, or I shall never get off at all.'

Then hesitation vanishes. Where he goes I must go. In hideous mockery the words of the Moabite woman flit through my mind, ' Whither thou goest, I will go.'

' I hear that Buenos Ayres is a most sociable place,' says Bryan, turning out his drawers pell-mell on the floor; 'plenty of gaiety always going on, and people very ready to make friends without asking inconvenient questions. How provoking! I ordered a lot of new ties the other day, thinking it as well to be prepared, and now I don't know where that fellow has put them.'

# CHAPTER XXXVIII

## FLIGHT

TAP, tap at my door, ten minutes later. 'May I come in?' cries Frances. 'Quick, unlock, open! I have such a piece of news for you!'

Strutting gaily in, eyes sparkling, cheeks glowing, mouth smiling, holding out the skirt of her habit in both hands, she makes a low curtsey at the reflection of herself in my long glass, while I re-lock the door behind her.

'Enter the future Mrs. Johnstone! Johnstone! Bah! How plebeian, isn't it? I have always laughed at double-barrelled names, but now I shall sigh for one. If I had only had some money we could have called ourselves Nugent-Johnstone, but it would be too ridiculous as it is.'

Then, taking off her hat, she goes close up
to the mirror and examines herself critically.

'I *am* looking nice to-day. I don't
wonder he came up to the scratch. How do
you think he did it, Esmé? He actually made
a speech—a regular oration. I can tell you
every word. It was just outside Charity
Wood, and the hounds were drawing——
What's this? Where are you going?'

For, turning away from the mirror, she
knocks against the small portmanteau which
I have been hurriedly filling with necessaries.
I open my lips to answer her; but the words
will not come.

'What has happened? How ghastly you
look, Esmé! Have you quarrelled with
Bryan? Ah! I see—I know! You are going
off to Allan Vaudrey! Thank Heaven I came
back in time to stop you!'

Again that tight grip at my throat; but I
know what it means now; I must not begin
to laugh. Only, what a funny mistake Frances

has made! No, I am certainly not going to
Allan; I am going away from him, from home,
from self-respect—to a place where the people
never ask inconvenient questions! Ha! ha!

'For, stop you I will,' goes on Frances;
'even if I tell Bryan——' she pauses; for
Bryan himself appears at the door between our
rooms, bearing triumphantly aloft a whole
pile of white waistcoats.

'I have found them!' he cries. 'Such a
comfort, isn't it? One can't enjoy anything
if one's clothes are too heavy. Oh! Frances!'

And he drops his bundle all in a heap.

'So you are packing too,' she says slowly,
eyeing us, first one and then the other. 'You
might tell me where you are going, I think.
It would be only polite.'

'You tell her please, Bryan,' I say
shakingly.

'We are going *away*,' begins Bryan with
great dignity and equal vagueness; 'and we
are sorry not to be able to ask you to come

with us, Frances.' Then, picking up his scat-
tered articles of attire, he adds hurriedly,
'The fact is, I have had considerable losses,
and it is just as well you should not know
where we are going——' and vanishes pre-
cipitately.

Frances is never one of those provoking
people who require everything to be explained
at full length ; a wink is always as good as
a nod to her, and with half a dozen quick
questions she has probed the whole situation,
and knows as much as I.

'You must not go with him,' she declares
in a low, hurried whisper ; 'you must stay
behind and brave it out. Everyone will
believe that you were kept in the dark about
his affairs, and no one will blame you.' Then,
throwing herself on her knees before me, she
flings her arms round my waist. 'Poor
darling Esmé ! I am so sorry for you ! '

In the midst of the overwhelming despair
that is crushing me, my sister's touch of affec-

tion comes like a ray of comfort. I shall always be glad that she spoke to me with such prompt love, and I shall like to remember that she wanted to keep me with her. Dear, pretty, bright Frances! I may never see her again.

Yet as I bend over her and, dry-eyed, kiss her upturned face, I know too well that I have only to touch one chord to make her relax all opposition to my flight.

'I must go with him, my pet; and it is better for you that I should. People will be kinder to you if you are left quite alone and not associated in any way with my disgraced name.'

Even as I speak her arms drop from me, and her ready brain begins mapping out her plans.

'I can stay with Mrs. Stuart,' she reflects aloud; 'and I don't think Major Johnstone will throw me over. How thrice providential that he proposed to-day!'

'Esmé!' calls out Bryan from the next

room, ' come here, and give me your opinion about these boots.'

From the depths of some recess he has unearthed about twenty pairs of boots of various sorts and descriptions, and has ranged them neatly in a row down the centre of the room, from window to door.

'I shan't want these, shall I?' he asks doubtfully, touching a pair of new top-boots. 'I don't think there is any hunting out there. I have never heard of any foxes at the River Plate, have you?'

His face is flushed, his eyes wandering, his hair disordered; with twitching hands he plucks at the front of his coat, and nervously opens his watch every two minutes. The three large portmanteaus he has selected to carry his wardrobe still gape in reproachful emptiness.

To catch the express at Swindon we must leave the house in half an hour. Bryan will never be ready if left to his own devices. I must pack for him and Frances for me.

So, on my knees before the first and largest of the leathern trio, I endeavour to reconcile space and time with Bryan's determination to be comfortable at Buenos Ayres. He clings desperately to the various knicknacks which embellish his dressing-room, and is specially attached to the fittings of his toilet-table.

'You know it is all very well for you to talk, my dear,' he remarks, waving a little silver hand-glass as he stands over me; ' but one can't get these things out there for love or money. And you will wish then you had shown a little more foresight.'

'How dare you speak to her like that?' breaks out Frances angrily. She has quickly and deftly finished my packing, and now stands watching my struggles with Bryan. 'Just look what you have brought her to! Poor, beautiful darling! Oh, what a fatal mistake we made when she married you!'

Bryan turns furiously upon her—he has always hated Frances; but in a moment I am between them.

'Come and help me put on my cloak, Frances; and, Bryan, you ring for the servants to take the luggage down. It is ready now.'

In two minutes my travelling things are huddled on, and Frances ties a thick veil over my quivering, tell-tale face. As we open the bedroom door we tumble against Julie and one of the housemaids, who are doubled outside with ears suspiciously near the keyhole.

'Julie, go and tidy up in there,' says Frances calmly. 'Madame has heard most distressing news; a dear relative is dying, and Madame goes to watch beside her sick bed.'

'Ah! Ah! C'est comme ça?' ejaculates Julie, with polite incredulity, but marches into my room nimbly enough. Her time for looting will be short. Frances will hurry upstairs the moment we drive off, and then Julie will have to play second fiddle.

The brougham is waiting, and my husband stands by the door.

Fear is not at any time an ennobling or beautifying emotion ; and to-day it has chased all vestiges of respectability from Bryan's person. He cowers beneath Dixon's fixed stare, and timidly inspects his muddy boots, turning his foot with unconscious mechanism first to one side and then to the other. Unwashen from the accumulated smuts of London and the train, his greasy skin dirtily shining, his clothes all awry, every line of his fat limp body betraying the nervous tremor which is shaking him, the whole aspect of the creature proclaims guilty cowardice, contemptible want of pluck.

Suddenly and horribly my heart quails within me. I cannot go with that man. I cannot follow him to be an outcast on the face of the earth.

I throw my arms around my sister and hold her tightly to me. In that desperate embrace I cling not to Frances individually, but to the old life of which she is the momentary embodiment.

'I cannot, Frances! I cannot!' I gasp breathlessly in her ear.

But though she responds warmly to my kisses and answers my tears with her own, her fingers unloose my convulsive clasp, and her hand guides me gently to the carriage. Frances is sorry for me ; but I should be decidedly in her way if I remained behind.

She need not have been afraid. My will is fixed, though for one moment my strength failed me.

# CHAPTER XXXIX

## DEAD

TRAVELLING across country by a local train, we have caught the express at Swindon, and are now flying rapidly through the high hedgerows and banked up ditches of placid, garden-like Berkshire.

Exhilarated by the motion and fortified by the sense of near escape from his troubles, Bryan is beginning to pluck up heart again. In the far corner of the carriage to which he has retreated he has made himself as comfortable as circumstances will permit; his feet rest on a handbag, a fur rug is wrapped around his knees, and as he polishes the silver mountings of his travelling flask with a very dirty pocket-handkerchief he even feels himself equal to whistling snatches of 'The Mikado' under his breath.

I am feigning sleep in order to get a little quiet. After attending carefully to my creature comforts, Bryan became extremely conversational, and began to amuse himself with wondering what our quondam neighbours will say when they hear of our flight.

'Mrs. Westby will declare that she feared it all along,' I have assured him wearily. 'Do you mind my resting now, dear? I think I shall go to sleep.'

So, with closed eyelids, I am left to my own reflections.

They say that to a drowning man a vision of his whole life swiftly appears, that events long forgotten rise up and flash across his memory. So to me, in the crisis of my fate, a panorama spreads itself out in which I see myself in various guises, from toddling happy childhood to the uneasy misery of my married life.

I am back again in spirit at Billington, and Frances and I are wandering about the beautiful gardens, or rambling through the fine great rooms full of time-honoured treasures, so different in their ancient stateliness from the modern glories of Milbourne. How we used to talk about our future husbands even when we were little chits in the nursery! Frances always declared that she would marry a duke, and from her tenderest years had well-defined notions as to which of his numerous places she would more particularly make her own. The lovers who existed in my imagination were legion, and varied in nationality, rank, and complexion. I have constructed romances, with myself for heroine, in which an emperor knelt before me, or in which I tramped barefooted through African deserts with a dusky Arab who had carried me off on my long-tailed steed—according to the last book approved by my fancy.

Then, as we grew older and went out in the

world, how its pleasures took hold of us! How quickly we picked up its jargon and apprised everything at its valuation! How highly we estimated our charms, and how lofty was the standard of our deserts!

I remember when Allan Vaudrey first came about me that I flirted with him and talked to him with a decided sense of condescension.

Fool that I was! Poor, motherless, misguided fool, who did not even know the A B C of my own heart. Of all I have left behind me at Milbourne, I most regret that little pencil-case of Allan's, thrown sturdily into the big pond in an access of combatant virtue. I wish I had kept it. If I had only known that I was soon to be torn away from all possible chance of seeing him again, I might have permitted myself to treasure that one little trifle that had belonged to him, that his hands had touched. He kissed my lips once—and furtively I put up my fingers and stroke them tenderly—but pah! how often has Bryan kissed them since?

Now I shall be as one dead to Allan. I used to think a week ago—yesterday even—that my life was broken, that I should never look in his eyes and hear his voice again. But I know now, in the lurid light of this supreme despair, that I was harbouring a lurking hope that he would come back to me, would yield to my conditions and brighten my days with his friendship.

Where I am going he can never follow me. Will he even know in what part of the weary world I am hiding my disgraced head, I wonder? Will our destination ever be mentioned in polite society? I suppose the detectives and all the people whom we have robbed will find out what uncivilised region is harbouring us from the grip of a just law, but our whilom friends and acquaintance will scarcely care to pursue their inquiries beyond the one word ' absconded.'

'By Jove! I have just remembered your picture!' exclaims Bryan. 'Blakely promised to send it home yesterday. I am sorry to leave it behind. Do you remember how I insisted upon the canvas being smaller than he wished? I had my reasons, you see. I always meant to take it with us.'

And he pauses for approbation of his fore-thought.

'How we are flying along!' he continues, as I make no reply. 'We must be going eighty miles an hour. They were late at Swindon, so I suppose we are making it up now.'

'Oh God! Thy hand is heavy upon me. Have mercy, and take away my life. I can endure no more. Surely the punishment for my offence is great. Have I not suffered enough to earn the repose of the grave? Have pity, and let me die!'

So I pray in utter desolation. Who would live without hope? And what hope can I

nave, doomed to wander an exile among the
scum of the earth, my husband my sole companion—a thief! Without remorse for the
past or anxiety for the future, he sits there
chuckling in childish short-sighted glee at his
present brief success.

I believe God will hear my prayer. I do
not think I shall live long. I have been feeling so weak lately; and in a hot climate,
with poor lodging and coarse fare, I shall
surely——

Crash! A hideous, grinding, tearing
noise.

The train is rocking, swaying wildly to
and fro. I am thrown against the opposite
seat, backwards, forwards.

Good God! This is some frightful accident! We are still rushing madly on, but
with what horrible violence we are shaken,
rattled, tossed about! Oh! if it would only
come quickly!—the awful smash which must
come! This agony is so long—so long!

The air is full of fearful noises—of wood and iron cracking, breaking, and above all the terrified shrieks of human voices. Bryan is screaming. For myself I know not if I cry out, but my eyeballs are straining in my head.

A shock more violent yet, which seems to lift me high in the air—and then, for one brief moment, stillness.

I am roused by steam rushing over me. I must get out of this horrible prison before I am scalded to death. Quick! Out of the window up there ! The carriage is turned on one side and the window high above me ; but I clamber over the arms of the seats. I push myself through the opening without waiting to clear away the broken glass ; I jump on to a bank of gorse, and tear my way up the high embankment—up, up to the very top, right away from that awful train, that blinding steam.

Then I fall upon my knees and pant aloud,

' Thank God, thank God ! ' full of gratitude in that it has pleased Him to spare the life that five short minutes ago I was beseeching Him to take.

Bryan has not followed me.

I rise from my knees and approach the edge of the embankment. What is this streaming wet upon my face and trickling down my neck? I put up my hand and withdraw it—red with blood. There, all down the front of my cloak is a stream of blood. Ugh ! I am bespattered with it all over. I must have cut myself getting through the broken window, for my limbs are safe and sound. Wildly I run my fingers over my head, my face, my neck. No, I can find no cut. My skin is scratched and torn indeed with the thorny gorse, but there is nothing on me to account for this hideous stream of blood. Why is Bryan not getting out of that fearful carriage? I must go and help him.

Trembling I crawl down through the gorse again.

The train is lying wrecked before me. Groups of people stand, sit, lie about, some screaming, some palely silent.

There is no one around our carriage. I remember that we came high up in the train near the engine so as to get a compartment to ourselves. The guard passes me running along.

'Stop!' I cry, full of shuddering terror. 'Stop! I want you to help me.'

'I cannot,' he replies, not slackening his speed. 'My own arm is broken, but I must stop the down express.'

Will no one come? There is a man down there, walking slowly towards me, but I cannot wait for him. Bryan may be wanting help.

Shaking violently in every limb I climb with difficulty up the carriage and on to its overturned side. I look through the broken window.   In the far corner, a shapeless, crumpled-up heap, Bryan is lying perfectly still.

.          .          .          .          .

Nothing can be done for him, they tell me.   He is dead !

# CHAPTER XL

## THE FUTURE

THEY take me to a farmhouse close by, and there the farmer's wife undresses me and puts me to bed, in spite of my angry remonstrance that I am quite well. I think she was right, though, for I remember that when she left me unsupported for a moment my head felt so strangely heavy that I could not hold it up, and my feet slipped away from me.

Once having got me flat the poor woman is at an end of her resources, and in helpless alarm gazes at me as I cry out, and moan, and shiver. It is apparently a relief to her when I exclaim crossly that my feet are like ice and my head like fire. These physical woes she can understand and alleviate.

It is not till far on in the night that I take any notice of her inquiries for the address of my friends, that she may communicate with them.

At first, nothing better has occurred to me than to turn my head fretfully away, but roused at last by her repeated declarations that I should feel quite well and happy if only 'my mamma, or my sisters, were to come and cheer me up,' I start wildly in the bed, and gripping her arm, scream out—

'There is no one who would come to me —no one. You don't understand. I am disgraced and quite alone!'

Whereupon she lifts up my left hand with an anxious frown, and is obviously reassured by the sight of my wedding-ring.

'I am very sorry to give you all this trouble,' I sob apologetically, 'and I will try to lie quiet now. But there is no one to whom you can write.'

Next day the doctor comes, evidently

upon her anxious representation that there must be something wrong with me internally, and makes an exhaustive examination of my wretched body.

He finds nothing amiss, and departs without even leaving a prescription, much to poor Mrs. Silwood's disappointment.

'I think if he had given you one of them nice fizzing draughts, it would have done you good,' she says regretfully, with the faith of her class in a medicine bottle.

Then she makes me get up and lie upon the sofa in her little sitting-room; and, the doctor having guaranteed the soundness of my various limbs and organs, sees no good reason why her curiosity should not be satisfied, and my mind exercised by a full, true, and particular account of the accident.

'We have always sworn that Flying Dutchman would run off the lines someday,' she begins contentedly; 'and to think it should have happened at our own door!

And what was the very last words your poor good man said to you, my dear?'

The horrible nightmare-like day is over at last, and as twilight closes in I lie in an exhausted and fitful slumber. Even in my sleep I retain consciousness of my troubles, and dream restlessly that Bryan's mother has no food in the house, and that my dressmaker keeps asking for her money. Then Jacquetta gets mixed up in it somehow; she must have come to see Bryan's mother, I suppose.

'I think you are quite right,' she is saying. 'A wretched fly like that would shake her to pieces.'

Why, that *is* Jacquetta's voice! I am not dreaming. In another moment I am folded in her comfortable embrace.

'Oh! You don't know all, Jacquetta,' I cry loudly, pushing her away. 'You don't know all, or you would never have come to me.'

'Yes, I do, dear. Hush! It is not your

fault,' she answers soothingly, as one would speak to a child. 'I have come to take you home with me. And who do you think I travelled with from Paddington? Why, Sir Allan Vaudrey! He saw the account of the accident in the morning papers, and came straight down from the North. No, you must not try to sit up, darling. Lie still and I will tell you what I am going to do. I am going to stay here with you to-night, and then to-morrow morning we will go home together, you and I. Sir Allan has gone away to order a comfortable carriage for you.'

.    .    .    .    .

Winter has given place to summer, and six months have drawn their veil over the troubles and horrors of that fearful January day.

I am lying in a hammock in Sir Joseph Yarborough's garden, a hammock slung by a cunning hand under the shadiest of copper beeches. The air is scented with the thousand odours of July; the roses are blooming around me in many-tinted profusion; the bees are humming their industrious refrain—are they making love, I wonder, or only commenting on the qualities of the wall fruit?

At my feet Jacquetta's Dachs is curled in dreamless slumber—Dachs is devoted to a hammock; in my lap lie half a dozen flowers and a French novel; over my head a Japanese parasol unnecessarily supplements the shade of the beech's lovely red leaves—and by my side sits Allan Vaudrey.

'It is so absurd to talk of the customs of society,' he is grumbling. 'We might as well be married now as in ten years' time. You and I are not going to lead conventional lives.'

'What a recklessly profligate statement!'

'Well, I stick to it. There is nothing conventional about the whole thing.'

'It certainly is not the custom of society for a man to pay the debts of his wife's first husband,' I reflect gravely.

'You needn't hark back to that again,' interrupts Allan. 'You make me feel sometimes as if I had bought you.'

'So you have,' I rejoin placidly. 'You have bought me with hard cash paid down on the nail to Bryan's creditors. I never would have married you or any other man if all those poor people had been swindled out of their money.'

'Well, now that all those poor people, as you call them, are satisfied, you might marry me at once.'

'I should like a long, *long* time first,' I rejoin absently, dropping my parasol and staring up into the leafy screen above me.

'You are not very polite,' says Allan in a mortified voice.

'It seems as if it would take me years and years to get over the deadly shame,' I continue.

'Nonsense! There's no shame about it! People only know that there were money difficulties, and as all claims have been paid in full no one can say a word.'

'I didn't mean that. I was not thinking of money just then. I meant the shame of having been Bryan's wife. Not Heaven itself can change that now, and I can never forget it.'

'Yes, you will forget it in time,' says Allan gently. 'Look what even six months have done for you. You are picking up wonderfully. You are getting quite plump,' lifting my hand before my eyes.

'Oh! I am much better than I was, of course. Let go my hand, Allan, quick!—there's a gardener coming round the corner.'

'There is one thing I have fully made up my mind about,' declares Allan presently. 'That odious sister of yours shall never set foot inside our doors. You don't want to see her, do you?'

'It doesn't matter much whether I want to see her or not,' I reply with a shamefaced

laugh. 'As Major Johnstone only carried out
the engagement on condition that she held no
communication with me, and as I was not
even asked to the wedding, he is not likely to
allow her to stay with me.' The contact would
be too contaminating.'

'Impertinent brute!' roars Allan angrily.
'He will have some new lights upon Frances'
character before long if I am not much mis-
taken. Serve him right too.'

'I dare say he will relent in his severity
when I am really and truly whitewashed by
marrying you, but in the meanwhile he thinks
it is better to be cautious.'

'Let me tell you, I will never have her
inside our doors! There!'

'Is this the cloven hoof of authority?' I
ask lightly, raising myself on my elbow to look
at him. 'You don't cherish any old-fashioned
notions about wifely obedience, do you?
Because I haven't the remotest intention of
obeying you—ever—about anything!'

'Well, that's fair notice beforehand.'

'You see,' I continue explanatorily, 'I always used to be very polite and obedient to Bryan because I didn't care for him—poor fellow! But I intend to do *exactly* as I like with you.'

'You are certainly getting better,' says Allan. 'That sounds almost like your old self again!

THE END.

PRINTED BY
SPOTTISWOODE AND CO., NEW-STREET SQUARE
LONDON

# NEW AND UNIFORM EDITION

OF

## THE COMPLETE WORKS

OF

# ROBERT BROWNING.

*In Sixteen Volumes, small crown 8vo., price 5s. each; or, in uniform set binding, price £4.*

This Edition contains Three Portraits of Mr. Browning, at different periods of life, and a few Illustrations.

There is also a Large Paper Edition of 250 Copies, printed on Hand-made Paper. This Edition can only be obtained through Booksellers.

London: SMITH, ELDER, & CO., 15 Waterloo Place.

# POPULAR NOVELS.

*Each Work complete in One Volume, price Six Shillings.*

**ROBERT ELSMERE.** By Mrs. HUMPHRY WARD,
Author of ' Miss Bretherton ' &c.

**RICHARD CABLE:** the Lightshipman. By the Author
of 'Mehalah,' 'John Herring,' 'Court Royal,' &c. Crown
8vo. 6*s.*

**THE GAVEROCKS.** By the Author of ' Mehalah,'
' John Herring,' 'Court Royal,' &c. Crown 8vo. 6*s.*

**JESS.** By H. RIDER HAGGARD, Author of 'King Solomon's
Mines' &c. Third Edition. Crown 8vo. 6*s.*

**THE GIANT'S ROBE.** By F. ANSTEY, Author of
' Vice Versâ ' &c. Crown 8vo. 6*s.*

**OLD KENSINGTON.** By Miss THACKERAY. Crown
8vo. 6*s.*

**THE VILLAGE ON THE CLIFF.** By Miss
THACKERAY. Crown 8vo. 6*s.*

**FIVE OLD FRIENDS AND A YOUNG**
PRINCE. By Miss THACKERAY. Crown 8vo. 6*s.*

**BLUE BEARD'S KEYS, and other Stories.**
By Miss THACKERAY. Crown 8vo. 6*s.*

**THE STORY OF ELIZABETH; TWO HOURS;**
FROM AN ISLAND. By Miss THACKERAY. Crown 8vo. 6*s.*

**MISS WILLIAMSON'S DIVACATIONS.** By
Miss THACKERAY. Crown 8vo. 6*s.*

**MRS. DYMOND.** By Miss THACKERAY. Cr. 8vo. 6*s.*

**LLANALY REEFS.** By Lady VERNEY, Author of
'Stone Edge' &c. Crown 8vo. 6*s.*

**LETTICE LISLE.** By Lady VERNEY. With 3 Illustra·
tions. Crown 8vo. 6*s.*

London : SMITH, ELDER, & CO., 15 Waterloo Place.